T0095478

The Love from Just One

MICHAEL WILLIAMS

Order this book online at www.trafford.com
or email orders@trafford.com

Most Trafford titles are also available at major online book retailers.

Printed in the United States of America.

ISBN: 978-1-4669-5775-6 (sc)
ISBN: 978-1-4669-5777-0 (hc)
ISBN: 978-1-4669-5776-3 (e)

Library of Congress Control Number: 2012918821

Trafford rev. 12/07/2012

 www.trafford.com

North America & international
toll-free: 1 888 232 4444 (USA & Canada)
phone: 250 383 6864 ♦ fax: 812 355 4082

Contents

✠

I would like to dedicate this book to my late grandmother, Mae Nell Kelley, for inspiring me to write this book. She was a great influence in my life in helping to guide me to the place in Christ I am in today. I based the character Big Momma Mae Nell Harris off my grandmother because she was the first Christian example I was exposed to that helped me see the love of God firsthand not only in what she said, but also through her actions. From all the advice she gave and all the actions I saw, I knew from a young age that I wanted to follow Christ but was scared to do so. She, along with other influences in my life, helped me see that I could be unashamed of the Gospel of Jesus Christ and live without any regret if I walked with God. I know one day I will watch my grandmother read this book in heaven and be proud of me for everything that I chose to accomplish with the help of God. Grandma, I dedicate this book to you; and may the character, with her actions and words I represented as you, bless someone as they have blessed me and the rest of your family.

In loving memory of Mae Nell Kelley; you finally made it home in 2009.

Foreword

The holiday seasons are filled with a special love and care from your family and friends. The smell of a freshly cooked smoked ham, collard greens, buttery corn bread, savory roasted turkey, and the well-known candy yams covered with a marshmallow glaze all kick off the holiday seasons starting on Thanksgiving Day. Then there's Christmastime, celebrating the birth of our Lord and savior Jesus Christ and the joy of having your family members you haven't seen for at least a year, all coming from different parts of the country just to spend one morning opening gifts and sharing stories from past Christmases. If I had to pick, I'd say that this is by far one of the best times of every year, at least for me. Some of the stories can be so embarrassing that they are only meant to be shared between family and close friends or anyone whom you consider family.

And last but not least, New Year's Eve. The day when the entire world sits back in anticipation, waiting for the New Year to begin. Whether you're looking at the TV waiting for the ball to drop in New York City or at church praising God in to the New Year, you just can't wait until the last ten seconds before the New Year just to start over. This is also the last time of every year when you gather with your family and friends, sharing more stories; but this time, it is about what you would do differently if you could take it all back or what you want to do that you've never done before. Some like to call it a New Year's resolution, meaning it's time to make a change in their lives—but I like to call it "the Decision." But one thing I've never understood is why some people think that they should wait until the

New Year just to make a change. Why not do it when you first get the urge? I mean, either way, when you decide on the change, make sure it's for the better—not just for yourself, but for others around you as well, because you never know how you might impact someone's life.

I'm Michael Harris and this is my story. The holiday season in 2004 was just eight years ago and was unlike any other I've ever had. I mean, the highlight of that year's season was not centered solely on everything I've just told you about. This particular holiday season was filled with disasters that turned to wonders and miracles, which I had only heard about from one of the older saints at my home church in Barstow, California. I always had the chance to hear a few stories every Sunday morning after Sunday school. These stories were from a very wise old gentleman named Lanier Bennett, (whom I call Pops) who was fifty-eight years of age those eight years ago. He would frequently tell us young kids jokes, always making us laugh until one of us would cry from the laughter. But for the most part, he would talk about how good God is and how He had these angel encounters. While there were many stories he would tell, there was one story he told us about one of his angel encounters that had always stuck in the center of my mind even today. Now I was a young kid, at only twelve years of age, so just hearing about angels is a big deal. But hearing about actual encounters from people whom you look up to was an entirely different ball game.

This particular story happened thirty years ago, with Bennett and his friend coming out of a store in San Francisco, California, back in the summer of 1974. They had just finished shopping and were walking to Pops' vehicle, an old silver Toyota van, ready to leave and go get gas before driving home. After reaching the van and unlocking the door, a man, whom some would call a transient or homeless, came out of nowhere and asked Pops for fifty cents.

After I heard fifty cents I'm thinking to myself, *Why in the world would anyone ask for only fifty cents? You can't do anything with fifty cents.* Because I was only a little tyke, I didn't know that fifty cents was a lot more back then, because I was only able to buy one bar of chocolate with it.

Now since he was having a bad day, Pops was extremely bothered by the man who was begging for money. He told the man, "Go away, I don't feel like being bothered right now." After he saying that, Pops and his friend immediately entered his van and drove off. After driving about five minutes down the road, he and his friend pulled off into a gas station to fuel up. When he opened his door and exited the van, the exact same man was standing in front of him and once again politely asked, "Do you have fifty cents?" Pops was confused shortly after seeing the man, asking himself, *Is this the same guy?* Then recognizing there was no way that any normal man or person for that matter could have traveled so far in such a short amount of time, Pops gave the man fifty cents.

Pops had remembered a scripture in the Bible that talks about being careful of how you entertain a stranger because you just might be entertaining an angel. If he hadn't remembered the scripture, he might not have given the man the fifty cents that he didn't even need. God tested his will to give, and even though it took the remembrance of scripture to get him to be generous, he still gave to a man who looked to have needed the fifty cents a lot more than he did.

Every time I hear this story, I would start to think about the possibility of the man taking off, running immediately after Pops drove away. Either that or the man had a twin. Either way I had no idea; I was only twelve with a very fascinating imagination. But nonetheless, every time I hear it, I always thought to myself, *I would love an opportunity like that to be in the presence of an angel.* My only fear is that if God did test me, I wouldn't pass with flying colors.

Now growing up as a child, I didn't have everything I wanted. But let's face it, my mom always made sure me and my two brothers, Shawn and Isaiah, had everything we needed. But now that my oldest brother Shawn is married and my brother Isaiah has moved out of our grandma's house, I'm now here by myself taking care of our grandma and the house alone at the age of twenty. My grandmother, Mae Nell Harris, or you can call her Big Momma, is a wonderful woman who loved God and all of His people with the entirety of her heart. There was never a time that she didn't go out of her way to pick someone up for church, buy something for one who was in need, or even let someone stay the night at her house. It was God who gave her the strength and the mind to carry on. She would always tell us when we were younger, "You can only do what you can; the rest is for the Lord to take care of." But for the longest time I would always wonder, *How does God take care of something when we never see Him do so?* Then one day I found out. I kept thinking back to the eye-opening stories Bennett would tell the youth about the angels, and how in most cases the angels were sent to help us. Whether it was to save someone or just to say something to give encouragement, the angels in his stories were always around to help someone through a hard time and nothing else.

This is what brings me to the 2004 holiday season I mentioned to you earlier. Like I said, I was only twelve years of age at the time and I didn't notice all the wonders moving around me until someone told me. Most of my time was filled with watching basketball on TV after I did my homework, going on adventures with my two older brothers, or playing video games until my mom told me to get off. I always heard stories from my Big Momma about the people whom she would meet during her everyday kingdom business for God.

What is only the story of her life, she would choose to share with me when she got tired of chasing me around the house after I satisfied my sweet tooth with some sort of candy, cake, or ice cream. Each person's story was mostly sad; however, they would only seem to start that way. After my grandmother would share the wisdom with them about everything she went through, there was always a change in their lives almost immediately. It was amazing for me to hear how easy it seemed for her to help people. Then she later told me that it was because of God sending her the help that she needed to assist them.

There were so many people whom my Big Momma would help, including myself. While it may seem like common sense, the main person who needed Big Momma's guidance the most was my mom, Renee. She was someone who went through a lot, all because of her own doing. To me, it always seemed like she needed that one person who would be there for her even though she would never admit it. So what I decided to do was to take matters into my own hands. I would leave my mom notes scattered all throughout the house, making it seem like God was leaving them for her. Even though she figured out it was me on the first day, I still decided to keep dropping random notes from God because of the smile I would see on her face. After eventually moving away from Big Momma's house with my mom and my two brothers, Big Momma's diabetes was starting to affect her. I mean, it wasn't to the point where she was going to die, but it was still enough to make anyone who knew her for years get scared. My mom decided to go check on her every other weekend, which was great for me, because I loved going to see Big Momma and Pops whenever he came around for Sunday dinner along with others that were invited from the church. But all this boils down to my grandmother and how she cared about so many people. I just hope that one day God will fix my heart to be like hers.

Acknowledgments

First, I'd like to thank God for giving me the gifts of imagination, writing, and patience and for continually helping me find something I love to do. I could have been doing anything else but you kept my mind on what's important.

I'd also like to thank Paul Johnson for helping me come up with more ideas for the angel. Those few ideas were a great contribution to the completion of this book.

And to everyone who has supported me through the trying six months of writing, I thank you for believing in me when others doubted this book would make a difference.

Proverbs 16:9 (NKJV)

A man's heart plans his way: but the Lord directs his steps.

Chapter One

I Cannot See, but I Trust!

1 Peter 1:8 (KJV)

*Whom having not seen, ye love; in whom, though
now ye see him not, yet believing, ye rejoice
with joy unspeakable and full of glory.*

October 15, 2004

"Wake up!" Sarah said, her scenic smile dropping as she began to cry, trying to figure out what just happened to her husband Joseph. Sarah took a detailed look across his body and noticed there was no movement. She swiftly dropped to her knees and grabbed ahold of Joseph's left arm, trying for the pulse in his wrist; but there was nothing to give her hope. "Baby, get up, please!" she shouted, "I need you here with me, I don't know how I'll go on without you." The anxious crowd gathered around them inside the mall was astonished to see this young man fall to the ground. He dropped like he was paralyzed from the neck down and the breath in his body was snatched out of his lungs.

Out of nowhere, a man came gliding through the crowd to reach the spot where Sarah was. The man then knelt down across Sarah—on the other side of Joseph—and stretched his hand out toward her. He grabbed Sarah's right hand with his left, and placed his right hand flat upon the forehead of Joseph and then asked Sarah, "May I pray with you?"

Sarah observed Joseph's almost lifeless body and cried out in a distraught voice, "Lord why, why did this have to happen?"

The man said, "Everything will be fine." as he looked focused at Sarah in her tear-flooded eyes. The man bowed his head, closed his eyes, and began to pray. "Heavenly Father, we come to You right now as humble as we know how, asking from You an answer. We know not why this has happened so suddenly, but we ask for wisdom and understanding of what You are doing. The instance of this event that has just occurred with this young man is terrifying and astounding to us all, but most of all, his wife. The two of them have been serving You for some time now and we know that Joseph's time has not yet come."

The man continued to pray as Sarah opened her eyes and looked at him in amazement. She described him to be dressed in an all-white three-piece suit, wearing shiny leather white shoes on his feet. His hair was dark brown and his voice was powerful, like the beat of a bass drum. But she was unable to remember the features in his face. "Lord, please give Sarah the wisdom and understanding she needs right now, so that she may be able to wait this hurting time out. I ask that You fill her with faith, trust, hope, and strength, which she will need until You have done Your mighty work in their lives. In Your son Jesus's mighty and precious name we ask this of You, Amen."

At the end of the prayer, the paramedics came storming through the door, which caused Sarah to look where the noise had come from. The first paramedic that rushed through the mall doors hollered, "Where is he?"

"Over here!" Sarah shouted while hopping and waving her hand side to side.

The two paramedics rushed over to her, and the closest one to Joseph politely demanded, "Ma'am, could you please move so we can try and help him? We need as much space as possible to perform any necessary procedure."

Sarah did what she was asked and then looked over to where the man was seen last and noticed that he had suddenly vanished. She wasn't sure what to think as she said to herself, *I cannot see but I trust.*

Thirty-three minutes earlier, Joseph, a twenty-five-year-old light-skinned African American with short, light brown hair and a pair of glasses, was at home working on his book called, *Don't Stop Keep Moving.* The book he was working on is part one of a series of books he had titled *My Life the Battlefield.* His wife Sarah, was also twenty-five years of age, but liked to tease Joseph every year on his birthday that she is older than him by seven days. Sarah was a beautiful white woman with hazel eyes and had long, light brown curly hair with a red tint. She had called Joseph on his phone in hopes that the two of them could meet on her lunch break from work. She was the founder of a clothing store called *Generational Beauty,* with her own clothing line. "Can you meet me at the mall around noon?" Sarah asked Joseph.

He began to laugh because he was writing a part in his book where a little boy told his friend to meet him around noon; insisting they race to meet Jesus.

"What's so funny?" Sarah asked as she smiled, knowing it's something that would only make him laugh.

Joseph, still laughing silently, said, "Nothing babe. I'll meet you at the mall and I'll be there right at noon."

Sarah ran her fingers through her hair and said, "OK, I love you."

"I love you too." Joseph responded with a big smile.

After Joseph hung up the phone he stood up from his chair and then picked up his keys. Before walking through the front door he said, "Lord, I'm not going anywhere until I know you're with me." Joseph smiled, nodded, and walked through the door.

Minutes later, Joseph was driving to the mall and simply said, "Lord, I don't know what you're doing in my life, but just because I cannot see, doesn't mean I don't trust."

Four minutes passed by and Joseph arrived at the mall and parked his car. He exited his car and looked at the watch that he was wearing on his right wrist to see he has twenty-three minutes before noon. He began to walk to the front doors of the building, thinking of something nice but small he could buy for Sarah before she arrived. When he reached the doors, he extended his right hand to grab the handle. Right before walking through the door, he saw out of his peripherals a man on the left side of the mall entrance sitting down on a bench. Joseph let go of the handle after deciding to approach the man. "Excuse me sir," Joseph said, "how are you today?"

The man looked up at Joseph and said with a deep voice, "I am blessed, how about yourself young man?" Joseph was shocked to hear that particular response, but only because of the man's appearance. The man's hair was dark brown, or so it appeared because of what looked to be dirt covering parts of his hair. His clothes were tattered and torn as if he hadn't changed clothes in months after running through the wilderness.

Joseph began to smile as he said in a soft tone, "Wow! That is amazing. I don't mean any disrespect at all, but most people who are in your position wouldn't have ever answered with that reply."

The man said jokingly, "Oh, and what position is that?"

Joseph was embarrassed for his comment and stuttered while saying. "I . . . I'm sorry, I didn't mean it like that."

The man laughed, "That is quite all right, I see where you're coming from. But have you ever heard of the phrase, 'Don't judge a book by its cover?' You shouldn't be quick to judge anyone based off their appearance. I could be a millionaire that likes to dress down at times for all you know." Joseph smiled and the man said, "But like you said, most people wouldn't respond the way I did, but that's because they don't understand that God is still God anyhow. Each day I'm awakened is enough of a blessing for me to continue moving forward. I have not yet faced a challenge that I couldn't handle by the grace and the help of God."

Joseph thought to himself, *How could this happen to someone with such faith in God?* and then he says, "If you don't mind telling me, exactly why are you here? I mean, how did you get in this position?"

The man closed his eyes for a brief second; he smiled and said, "Well, I don't look at this as a position I'm stuck in. I can freely stand up and leave this place whenever I please, but I don't because God has a purpose for us all. He has one for you as well, and you'll find out what it is soon enough."

Joseph chuckled, "You aren't talking about sitting here are you?"

"Not exactly, you see God has something wonderful for you, and I can see that it is on its way as we speak. But there is one thing you do need to ask yourself and that is, will you be ready to receive it when it comes?"

Joseph smiled, looked at his watch, and then said, "I'll be ready when it's time. I have no doubt about that. But right now I have to be ready for a lunch date with my wife. I promised her I would meet her here at noon, but I need to pick up a gift for her."

"Is it a special occasion today?" The man asked.

Joseph replied, "Yeah, it's our anniversary. I would like to stay and chat for a bit, but unfortunately I don't have more time. Hopefully, we'll run into each other again."

"That's fine, go take care of your business and don't worry about me, I'll be OK. And as far as us two crossing paths again, I'm almost certain we'll be seeing each other again." The man began walking away as he nods, "Take care of your wife and God bless!"

Joseph looked into the parking lot after he thought he heard someone call his name, but there was no one there. He looked back to where the man was but he was no longer there.

"Thank You Jesus!" Joseph said as he opened the mall doors and walked inside. While inside, Joseph looked at his watch to see he only had 12 minutes left until Sarah was supposed to meet him. With the lack of time to really shop for a gift, besides the gift for her he had in the trunk of his car, he hurried to a flower shop and bought a dozen roses. Afterward he picked up a box of assorted chocolate and an anniversary card that reads, "Nothing in this world can replace the love that God has stored within you." Joseph read the card and thought to himself, *There's something missing.* Then he signed the card underneath the prewritten message. *I'll love you until the one fake rose I gave you dies.* At the instance of Joseph putting a full-stop at the end of the sentence, his phone rang. Joseph pulled the phone out of his front right pocket and saw it was Sarah calling.

"Hey baby! Where are you?" He answered.

"I'm entering the mall as we speak. Where are you?" Sarah asked.

"I'll meet you in the front. Can you wait for me next to the map right when you enter into the mall? I'm on my way. I'll be there as fast as I can."

Sarah told Joseph yes and waited for him to make his way to her. When Joseph was only four stores away from her, he started to walk faster. Sarah saw him as he was walking toward her with flowers and chocolate in hand. When he neared her he said, "Happy anni—" Right then, Joseph's heart had begun to beat a mile a minute. He immediately grabbed at his chest and forehead; his legs became weak and then he fell to the ground in an instant. Sarah dropped her purse as her hazel eyes opened wide. She ran the few feet over to Joseph, screaming, "Jesus! Somebody call 911, please!" Sarah started crying while she held Joseph around his shoulders with his back against her leg.

"Lord please, please help!" Sarah was worried and began talking to Joseph in a soft tone while she rocked slowly and stroking his hair.

"Everything will be all right! The Lord has it in control. There was never a battle that He has lost and this is a fact that we have come to know. Baby, hear my voice! I'm here with you and here to stay. Don't leave me now because I need you here always. God wants you here because you have work to do. The words that you're writing are so you can help people too. Stay strong, I know you can hear me, just come back soon so that you can see me. I love you Joseph!"

Immediately after the man came to pray, Sarah moved out of the paramedics' way when she was asked. The man was gone in what seemed to be a blink of an eye. When nothing was making a difference after trying everything they could, the paramedics decided to place him on the stretcher and wheel him to the ambulance. One of the paramedics pulled Sarah aside and said, "Are you this man's wife?"

Sarah replied. "Yes, do you have any idea of what's going on?"

"Well, right now, we aren't sure, but we're going to take him to the hospital right now for further treatment. Would you like to ride in the ambulance with him?"

"Yes." Sarah said with tears running down her face. Sarah and the paramedic that was talking with her quickly entered the back of the ambulance.

Once inside the ambulance, Sarah was eager to get to the hospital. When the IVs were being connected to Joseph's arms and tubes going in his nose, she got nervous because she had never seen anyone in a serious condition.

The paramedic in the back of the ambulance with Sarah saw her staring off into space, "How are you holding up?" He asked.

"I'll be OK." Sarah said. "I'm just a little worried."

"I'm sure he'll be fine. Try not to worry so much."

077

Different thoughts of what could happen began running through Sarah's mind, creating a dead silence. The only sound that was heard were the sirens of the ambulance, that is until the paramedic broke the silence with a random question, "How long have you two been married?" asked the paramedic.

Sarah didn't even smile halfway, but she still replied. "We've only been married for three years today. We've known each other since we were kids, growing up together and attending the same church."

"Is he a great man?"

"One of the greatest. I remember it took him forever to approach me, but when he finally did he was the sweetest and most honorable man I knew. He reminded me so much of my father when he was alive."

"I'm sorry to hear that about your dad. This must be hard for you."

Another silence crept up around them, and once again the paramedic broke the silence. "That is a blessing though, I mean the way the two of you met in church and now here you two are today still together. It sounds like a fairy tale in the making."

Sarah smiled this time, accepting the conversation that was brewing.

"Yeah, it is. He has never let me down once, even after all these years. God really answered my prayers when He sent my husband, and I thank Him every day and night when I pray."

The paramedic saw tears streaming from the corners of Sarah's eyes, and hands her a sheet of tissue paper to wipe her nose.

"Thank you." She said while becoming embarrassed. "I probably look a mess."

"Trust me, I'd be doing the same thing if my wife was in your husband's position."

"So you're married?"

"Yes, I am. Actually, my wife and I were recently married." He paramedic said.

"When was that?" Sarah asked.

The paramedic smiled as he looked down on the floor, "We've been married for almost 3 months now, and I've never been happier in my life since the day I met my wife." The paramedic continued to smile while he talked. "But do yourself a favor. Stay strong because your husband needs you to be that solid rock you have on your finger right now more than ever."

Sarah giggled a little while saying, "Thank you!"

The paramedic became confused and said, "You're welcome, but I'm not even sure exactly what I did."

"It's just nice to be smiling during such a hard time. God knows who to put in your path when you need it most, so thank you!"

"You're welcome. I hope someone would do the same for my wife if something ever happened to me." He paused briefly before continuing. "They're going to do everything possible at the hospital to keep him with us. The hospital has a great medical staff and plus, God is on his side."

"What's your name by the way?" Sarah asked.

"My name is Demetri Thomas, and my partner in there is Robert Brown."

"Well, Demetri Thomas, I'm Sarah, and I appreciate everything you and Robert are doing for my husband and me."

"You're welcome, we wouldn't think of doing anything less than what God wants us to do."

The ambulance came to a stop and began backing up to the double doors of the hospital's emergency room.

"OK we're here, let's go!" the lead paramedic, Robert, said to Demetri. The two of them locked eyes for a brief second, nodded at one another, and then jumped out of the ambulance. When they opened the back of the ambulance and pulled Joseph out on the stretcher, they proceeded forward through the double doors of the emergency room. Robert's eyes intensified because of his need to help Joseph as best he could. As soon as they're two feet into the building with Sarah trailing behind, a male and female nurse came to assist the two paramedics in bringing Joseph to a room. Sarah was asked politely by the female nurse if she could wait in the hall until they know what's going on with Joseph. She became frightened but still did as she is asked and began to wait.

"You'll be able to come in to the room immediately after we're done. Someone will come and get you as soon as we know something." The nurse said.

Sarah nodded and walked to the waiting room. Once inside the waiting room she called her store.

"Thank you for calling Generational Beauty, This is Jennifer speaking, how may I help you?"

"Hey Jennifer, it's me, Sarah."

"Hey boss lady, what can I do you for?"

Sarah's voice became choppy as she thought about what she was about to tell Jennifer.

"I was just calling to let you know that I'm going to need you to close the store tonight." Sarah said.

"Yeah, no problem, I can do that for you. Is everything all right?" Jennifer asked.

Sarah paused for a second and said, "Joseph is in the hospital."

A soft and short gasp erupted from Jennifer because of the unexpected news about Joseph.

"What happened?" Jennifer asked in a very concerned voice.

"All I know so far is that he passed out at the mall, I wouldn't be able to tell you any other details. But I will let you know as soon as I find something out. I'm going to try and come by the store later tonight."

"Are you sure? Maybe you should take the rest of the day off."

"Yeah, I will, I just need to pick something up that I bought him."

"Aw!" Jennifer exclaimed. "It just hit me that it's your anniversary today. I'm sorry you have to spend it alone." Jennifer paused shortly before she continued. "You know if you'd like, you could always come over and we can hang out?"

"Thanks, but I already decided to stay the night here at the hospital with Joseph so he isn't alone.

"OK, well, you take care, and if you need anything, just give me a call, OK?"

"I will" Sarah replied.

After the two of them hung up the phone, Sarah looked up toward the ceiling and said to herself, *Lord I need you now more than ever.*

Chapter Two

While I Sleep, He Speaks

Job 33:14-16 (KJV)

For God speaketh once, yea twice, yet man perceiveth not. In a dream, in a vision of the night, when deep sleep falleth upon men, in slumberings upon the bed; then he openeth the ears of men, and sealeth their instruction.

October 15, 2004

E ver since his untimely collapse at the mall, Joseph had been having a very interesting dream.

In the dream, Joseph was walking through the wilderness with his head looking straight down at the ground; his mind focused on following what he thought to be the Lord's instructions.

"You're almost there" said the Lord as Joseph was making his way out of the wilderness. Once out he saw a large lake stretching at least eight miles to the left and to the right, but only five miles across. When he reached the edge of the water he came to a stop, just inches away. Joseph looked down into the water which was unbelievably clear, and could see at least twenty feet below the surface. He took a step and then stopped before entering deep into the water, after he saw a light so bright that it lit up the entire sky. The light he saw was holding itself out afar across the lake on what looked to be a small island. After seeing the light, Joseph didn't even hesitate before taking a dive into the water. He was so focused on getting to his destination that he didn't notice the arctic jolt that shot through his bones from the tiny pieces of ice floating on its surface. Nonetheless, he still swam effortlessly through the spine-chilling water. In the midst of swimming, Joseph was suddenly being pulled down by a very strong force. Even with the water being practically visible to the bottom, Joseph was unable to see anything stopping him from swimming as fast and as strong as he normally could. But nonetheless he decided to push forward not letting anything hold him back. The struggle was tough but he knew for some reason he just had to get to that light. Halfway through the swim, Joseph began to lose his strength and it caused him to slow down. While he floated in the middle of the scene, a group of seventeen fish came out of nowhere and began to swim around him.

Joseph marveled at the fish as they swam around him, and he began to sink. Realizing he was being distracted, Joseph began to regain his focus and placed it back on getting across the water to where the light was. As he continued on swimming, Joseph began to lose strength in his body and slowly descended under the water; he asked God, "Lord, have you left me here alone to drown or have I just given up my will to fight? I can feel my strength slipping away as I pursue the destination which was set. I need you to give me more strength or help me so I can finish. I know that I cannot do this on my own."

Joseph swam up and once again began to swim forward using all the might he had left, but his effort was to no avail. At that moment of complete exhaustion, three of the fish that were swimming around him helped him across to the island. The three fish helped Joseph stay afloat while the other fourteen chose to swim around him and just to watch. Almost to the end, Joseph regained a portion of his strength and was able to keep himself from sinking, but the fish continued to help anyways. With his strength regained, Joseph began to swim on his own, and the fish swam away. Out of the three fish that were helping him, two chose to swim to the back of his feet and the third fish swam on his right side by his hand.

Twenty-two feet away from the land where the light was, Joseph looked and saw he was almost there. After he reached the knee high water, Joseph was breathing heavily from the swim but he slowly moved toward dry land.

Joseph collapsed to his knees and he shouted, "Oh God!" as his face dropped down toward the earth. With water running down his face dripping off in to the ground, Joseph lifted his head and looked forward to see the light that he has been pursuing. As he slowly rose to his feet, using only his legs to give himself leverage, Joseph walked one step at a time toward the light. The closer he got, the farther it seemed to be; so he ran as fast as he could. As he was running, he began to run faster, and faster, and faster. He finally reached the light and came to a stop. Joseph held his right hand in front of his eyes to block the brightness of the light and then he paused shortly while gazing at the light which was only about a foot away. The light seemed to look like it surrounded the silhouette of a man. The silhouette was black with the light outlining it. The light was letting off a bright glow of gold; as Joseph gazed into the light, he began to reach out his right hand slowly toward it. As his hand got closer, the glow from the light wrapped around his arm and became a part of him. He swiftly pulled his hand away because he didn't know what the glow was. Joseph held his hand up in front of his face and moved it around as if it was in a showroom. Nothing was wrong with his hand so he reached further into the light for a second time . . .

Joseph's eyes opened and his vision was blurry. He sprung up breathing as if he was just under water holding his breath. He realized he wasn't wearing his glasses, but was still able to see he was in a hospital, lying in bed with tubes coming from his nose and arms. After Joseph saw his wife Sarah lying down sleeping peacefully in a reclined chair, he called her name.

"Sarah," he called but there was no answer. *She must be sound asleep,* Joseph thought to himself and decided not to bother her. She was holding a present tightly in her arms while she was waiting for Joseph to wake up. Joseph, not wanting to wake Sarah, decided to close his eyes as he tried to rest. Joseph wasn't able to go back to sleep, so he just laid in bed with his eyes closed and began to talk with God.

Half an hour later, Demetri, stepped through the door as he knocked. "Joseph." Demetri said hesitantly, not sure if he was asleep or not.

Joseph heard the knock and opened his eyes to see this young man who looked to be only a few years out of high school. "Yeah, come on in." Joseph replied pleasantly.

"Hi, I . . . I'm Demetri," he said while stuttering.

"Nice to meet you," Joseph responded, "Or do we know each other?"

"Yeah, we do, I . . . I mean not really. I'm one of the paramedics who helped bring you here to the hospital."

"You must be pretty nervous, unless your stuttering is just a habit? Joseph chuckled. "But thank you! I am very grateful for all you've done for me. If God hadn't sent you when He had, I don't know what would've happened to me."

"You're welcome, I'm just glad to be of some help. But I just wanted to come and check on you. To make sure you were recovering OK."

"I could be better, but I thank God I'm still alive to fight another day. How long have I been unconscious?" Joseph asked.

Demetri looked at his watch and was surprised to see how much time had passed. "Looks like you've been asleep closing in on five hours now."

"Wow really? I wouldn't have ever guessed as much. I mean, the dream I just had seemed so much longer. But I'll tell you one thing, I thank God it wasn't any longer, because I don't want to wake up and my child is growing up already." Joseph said with a hint of laughter in his voice.

"You have a child?" Demetri asked.

"No, not yet, but Sarah and I are expecting in about seven months." Joseph then had a smile stretching from ear to ear.

"Well, congratulations!" Demetri said. "And good thing you'll be out of here soon.

"Yeah, I know what you mean. It would be a sad day for a man to miss the birth of his child. But thank you, Demetri, that does mean a lot."

"So what about that dream of yours? I mean, would you mind telling me about it?"

"Yeah, I don't see why not. I can break it down for you real quick."

"Do you ever write down your dreams?"

"No, I've never thought of it."

"You should start. My dad used to have my brother and me write down our dreams just in case we forgot them down the road."

"So it was like insurance for interpretation?"

"Yes, exactly!" Demetri said after shaking his head and laughing. "It's not often God gives you a complete interpretation for a dream you know."

"Oh, I know what you mean. So where are your dad and brother at these days?"

Demetri became quiet as he thought about his dad and his brother's whereabouts.

Joseph saw Demetri's smile slowly fade away. "I'm sorry man, I shouldn't have asked about your family. You don't have to talk about them. It just crossed my mind is all."

"It's OK. I don't mind talking about them. It's just that it's been so long since I've talked about either of them." A short silence arose as Demetri paced two steps back. "So do you still want to hear about my dad? I really don't mind."

"Sure, let it fly."

"Well, my dad is a great man and was very hard working."

"Was? Did he pass away?"

"Yeah, he passed away five years ago. It was hard to deal with his death the first couple of years. It even came to the point where I didn't want to be here anymore."

"Did you attempt killing yourself?"

Demetri's eyes began to water just thinking about how his dad died. "Yeah, I . . ."

The hurt in Demetri's face became very apparent. "It's OK, you don't have to talk about it if you don't want to." Joseph said.

"No, it's OK, I need to. I've never talked with anyone about it."

"That's understandable, but what about your wife?"

"How did you know I was married?"

"Because of your ring."

Demetri smiled slightly, "That makes sense. But to answer your original question, I just never felt that I needed to. I've always been on my own up until I met my wife, Nicole. But can you believe I've only mentioned my dad around her once?"

"She doesn't ask about him?"

"She does, but she told me I could wait until I was ready to tell her."

"Maybe you should tell her."

"Yeah, you're right I should." Demetri agreed. "So what about this dream you had?"

Joseph told Demetri the dream from start to finish, not missing one detail. Demetri was amazed to hear the dream itself, but he was more amazed that Joseph remembered the entire thing.

"God has really blessed you. Are you sure you haven't missed anything?"

"Yeah, I'm pretty sure I told you the whole dream. I've always been able to do so, just ask my wife."

"Ask your wife what?" Sarah said.

When she finally woke up from her sleep, Sarah stood up and lifted the cover off her body while rubbing the sleep away from her eyes.

"I was just telling Demetri here that I remember everything I dream of." He explained.

"Yes, you do, but you seem to have a problem remembering other things that are important."

"Like what?" Joseph asked.

"Like you forgetting about our anniversary today."

"But I was sleep, well, sort of." Joseph said while smiling.

Sarah walked toward Joseph and presented the anniversary gift she brought for him.

"Happy anniversary!" Sarah said while handing him the gift.

Joseph smiled and thanked her for the gift. It was hard for him to see because of his vision without his eyeglasses. Demetri smiled while watching the two of them so happy together.

"Well, I'll leave you two alone now." Demetri interrupted. "Oh, and, Joseph, make sure to rest up for a few days no matter how good you may feel, and also, you need to stay hydrated. Last, if you need anything feel free to give me a call. I'll come as fast as I can."

"I will, and thanks again Demetri." Joseph said while Demetri gave him his phone number.

"Oh, and one more thing, when God gives you the interpretation of that dream I want to see it become reality."

Joseph looked at Demetri a little confused as if he already knew what the dream meant.

"What dream?" Sarah asked.

"I'll tell you about it later babe, and Demetri, whatever the dream stands for will come to pass if the Lord says the same."

"I'll hold you accountable to that." Demetri replied. He then turned and left the room while saying goodbye.

"It's nice to see you made a new friend, and a great one at that. Demetri is the one who stood by my side and kept a smile on my face when we were in the ambulance."

Sarah reached around Joseph's neck and held him as tight as she could.

"I didn't know what was going on, but thank God you're still alive." Sarah said.

"Just because I'm in this bed doesn't mean God has forgotten about me. For as long as I can remember I have been chosen by God, so I know He isn't going to let anything take me out of this world just yet."

"I hope not, because it was horrible to see you pass out while you were walking toward me. I almost wasn't sure how to react."

"Babe, the feeling of falling wasn't even there. It's almost like I just blacked out. Before waking up here I don't remember a whole lot."

Out of nowhere Sarah started to think of the man who came to pray with her.

"Something strange happened when you fell."

"Did your beauty make some other poor guy fall as well?" Joseph said with a smile.

"That isn't funny. I'm being serious right now. While I was kneeling by your side, some guy came out of the crowd and prayed with me."

"What's so strange about that?"

"The guy showing up to pray wasn't strange. The thing that was strange is after he finished praying, he was no longer there. It was almost like he was never there."

Joseph thought of the man whom he had encountered outside of the mall. "What did this man look like?" he asked.

"All I remember about him is he was wearing all white, his hair was a shade of brown and his voice was very deep. As for his face, I didn't really get a good look at it."

Now even though the description was not the same as the man Joseph had thought of, it was weird to him that the two men's profiles were about the same. Regardless of what Joseph thought, he still seemed to believe they were the same man.

"Really?" Joseph said. "God does say the prayers of the righteous will never be forsaken!"

Joseph decided to keep his thoughts to himself as Sarah continued on about the man from earlier.

"Babe, while he was praying, every word he said had power behind it."

"That reminds me of when my Youth Pastor Ryan Beal from back then said, 'It's good to know the power of prayer, but it's better to pray with power.'"

Sarah thought on those words, and because of the example seen and felt earlier she knew it was nothing but true.

"I would hate to think what could've happened if he wasn't there." Sarah added.

"Well, we should be thankful for how God turned things around. This may not have been the best outcome, but it is one that I seemed to have needed."

Sarah prays to herself, *Thank You God for helping him stay optimistic for the both of us.*

"All right baby," Sarah said while giving Joseph a kiss on his forehead. "I told Jennifer I would be at work tomorrow so I have to leave you for now. But I promise I will be back as soon as I'm off, OK?"

"Yeah, that's fine. I'll see you later, and hopefully I'll be able to get out of here when you arrive."

"Oh, and your doctor should be here soon. I spoke with him when I arrived and he told me that you'll have to stay overnight for at least one more day so they can run more tests to make sure you're OK."

"I was hoping I wouldn't have to but those are the doctor's orders." The two of them hugged tightly, and Joseph said, "Have a wonderful day at work, I love you!"

Sarah replied, "I love you too!"

Chapter Three

God Chose Me for This Job, But Why?

Proverbs 22:6 (KJV)

Train up a child in the way he should go: and
when he is old, he will not depart from it.

October 19, 2004

"Come on, come on!" Robert said in a panic. "Pick up the phone please!"

The sound of the annoying waiting ring was all Robert heard as he anticipated someone answering the phone. Ring, ring, ring, ring; the phone continued to ring even after he called for a second time, but once again there was still no answer. Because Robert wasn't sure of what to do he became frustrated and a little afraid.

What do I say? Robert thought to himself after there was no answer on the third and final time.

"Hi . . . um, this is Robert Brown." He starts the message. "I'm not sure if you will remember me, but I'm an old friend of Elise's." Robert said nervously. "I'm calling to see—" he paused to correct himself. "No, I'm calling because I need your help. If you know where Elise could be at or how I might be able to get in touch with her, I need you to return my call. I've called her sister and her mom already but neither one of their numbers seem to be connected. Anyways this is very urgent, so when you get this message can you please call me back as soon as possible? Once again this is Robert Brown." Robert hung up the phone and immediately thought to himself, *Did I leave my phone number?* Because he wasn't sure, he didn't hesitate to call back and leave a callback number.

Robert spoke out loud. "I don't understand!"

One hour earlier, Robert, a twenty-six-year-old African American male, wearing a black tank-top and white basketball shorts, heard a knock at his door. As he approached the door, he wondered who could be behind it. When he opened the door he found out it was his childhood friend and high school sweetheart, Elise Magnano.

Elise is a gorgeous Italian redhead with green eyes and a face you'll never forget. The first thing Robert noticed after he opened the door of his condo was Elise's pearly white smile. Immediately after, he saw her hand is holding the tiny hand of her son, who was only five years old. Robert couldn't believe his eyes after being stunned seeing Elise, who he hadn't been in contact with since they graduated high school six years ago.

"Hi, Robert, how have you been?" Elise said with an electrifying smile across her face.

Robert began to smile because he couldn't help but do so. The two of them go way back; from riding bikes together, all the way to being the first person either of them had fallen in love with. Stricken with fear of what could happen next depending on what he said, Robert spoke cautiously as if a bomb was about to go off.

"Elise, is that really you? I never thought I was going to see you again after all these years."

"I've always thought about visiting, but I've never had the time away from work and this little guy."

"So what have you been doing all these years?"

"I've been teaching."

"Teaching what?"

"I've been teaching fourth graders for the last three years."

"What happened after school?

"After we graduated I went off to college in Washington State; and soon after, I found out I was going to be a mother, as you can see."

"Yeah, I see" Robert replied, a little sarcastic. "He resembles you a lot."

"Thank you. He's been a blessing in my life. The feeling of watching him grow up before my eyes is indescribable. He reminds me a lot of my father, but even more of his."

Robert discarded all thoughts of the child after becoming irritated, and followed up with the question that had been on his mind since Elise arrived.

"So how did you find me?" He asked.

Elise could immediately tell that Robert was getting upset, so she explained herself as best she could.

"Let's just say it was hard to find you. Oh, and also tiring after searching all these years."

Why would you have searched for me after leaving me for someone else? Robert thought, but doesn't ask.

"There was a time I thought I wouldn't find you, until I saw your picture on the news. That's when I went to the hospital where you and your partner took that man who passed out in the mall. When I asked around I just happen to talk to the right people."

"I wish you wouldn't have looked for me," he stated.

"Why would I not?" Elise asked. "I hope you didn't think I didn't want to be in your life."

Robert was saddened at the thought and his voice softened, "Like I said earlier, I never thought I would ever see you again. I did my best to forget about you and when it finally happened I did."

"Why would you want to do that?" Elise asked curiously.

Robert ignored her question with a question of his own. "So why are you here?"

Elise's nerves built up, causing her eyes to slightly twitch, but it was almost unnoticeable. "What do you mean? I came to see you!"

Robert's heart hardened because he's afraid of Elise coming back to his life and leaving again.

"I don't believe it. Nobody just shows up at someone's house after all these years without so much as a phone call or receiving an invite. So just tell me what's going on, are you in trouble or something? Do you need money?" Robert asked with no hesitation.

Elise was dismayed and any happiness that was left in her was completely flushed out. Tears rolled down her face until it hit the floor.

"I told you, I came to see you. Why does it have to be more than that?"

Robert's voice intensified with resentment the more she spoke.

"Because I know you Elise. Did you forget we grew up together and that I know every single thing about you? Don't you think I'd know if you were lying to me?"

As soon as the two of them started to argue, Elise's son ran and hid in the bathroom; closing the door behind him because he was afraid.

"I think you should leave. I don't have time to deal with this right now. I still have to get ready for my shift tonight."

As shocked as she was to hear it, she still thought about whether she should tell him the truth of why she was there.

"OK I will, but I need you to do me a favor."

"Oh yeah, and what's that?" Robert asked as his eyes watered with anger.

Elise then had tears fall slowly down her face because of Robert's hurtful words. "I need you to watch my son."

"What, are you serious? And why is that?" Robert asked.

"I have something very important that I must to take care of and I need someone to watch him."

"I knew it was something. You should've asked your family instead of wasting time looking for me" Robert said in a loud tone.

"I wasted my time because you're the only one I knew around here that could take care of him."

"Well, you shouldn't have."

"I did, because I know you would do anything for someone, no matter who they are or what they've done."

Robert ignored her words and looked toward the front door, but Elise didn't care. Instead, she reminded him a little of whom she knew him as.

"I know you don't want me here, but do you remember that you were the one who saved me when I was drowning in the swimming pool? I know you're the one who took care of me as best you could, even though you had no idea of what to do. And I also know that you're the one who told me before I went off to college that if I needed anything, no matter how big or how small, you would go out of your way to help me if need be."

Robert yelled because he couldn't control the two emotions that had built inside, "I was young when I did and said that to you. And when I told you those things it was because I'm in—" Robert stopped after he thought about what he was about to say. "I used to love you and you know that, so of course I would say something like that. But when you decided to run off to be with some guy who obviously left you with a child to raise on your own, I had no choice but to do my own thing."

Elise looked at Robert, wondering if she was making the right choice.

"I couldn't tell you the truth." Elise said as she turned away from Robert and rushed out of his house without closing the door.

Robert followed after her out the door. "What truth?" He asked, but Elise never responded to his voice and continued to walk to the taxi. As he watched Elise leave, Robert mumbled to himself, "I'm sorry."

Robert was frustrated with himself because of how he handled the situation, so he slammed the door behind him and then walked back into the living room where he saw Elise's son coming from out of the bathroom. Robert's eyes widened and his jaw dropped after seeing the child with a curious look on his face. Robert practically ran through his door, causing it to bounce off the wall after he ran outside to catch Elise. Too bad though that she was long gone by the time he got out and walked to the middle of the street. Since she was gone, Robert ran back into the house and grabbed his cell phone off the coffee table to call her family members. After getting no answer from either Elise's sister Ashley or her mom, Robert called Elise's grandmother, Ms. Robinson, but there wasn't even an answer from her. Robert left a message on her answering machine and hoped for a return call.

"Oh shoot!" Robert said after realizing he's going to be late for work. *What am I going to do? I have to be at work in an hour and I still need to shower, get ready and drive thirty minutes to Barstow,* Robert thought to himself. Robert has lived in Victorville, CA, since he was hired as a paramedic immediately after he graduated from Barstow High in 2004.

After calling every person he knew that could possibly be able to watch the child while he's at work, Robert found that no one was available. He then called ahead at work to let his boss know that he would be at least five to ten minutes late. With only half an hour before his shift and 26 miles to drive, Robert showered quickly and was ready for work, but he was still puzzled as to what he could do with the boy. He walked over to the couch where the boy had fallen asleep and thought out loud, "Well, it looks like you'll be coming with me, but I have no idea of what I'm going to do with you."

While driving his white two-door convertible, Robert's cell phone began to ring. Unfortunately though, it rang when he was only five minutes away from work, and he was on track to be on time if all the traffic lights turned green. He pulled the phone out of his right pocket and was relieved to see that it was Elise's grandmother returning his call. Robert flipped his phone open to answer it, but by the time he pressed answer, it had already stopped ringing and Elise's grandmother was sent to voicemail. "I'll call her back when I get to work." Robert whispered to himself while placing the phone on his lap.

Seconds later, Robert came to a red traffic light where he was forced to stop. He thought about the danger but picked up his phone and listened to the voicemail Elise's grandmother left.

"Hello, I'm trying to reach Robert Brown. He called earlier and I was just returning the call." Robert exited his voicemail box and called her back. As the phone rang, the crossing traffic lights shift from green to yellow. Robert noticed the light is readying to change so he hangs up phone. While attempting to place the phone back in his pocket it fell on the floor next to the brake pedal. Robert reached for his phone, but without knowing, he was gradually pressing the accelerator and the car inched toward the intersection. There were only a few cars left that could cross legally as Robert's car slowly moved past the crosswalk on their side of the street.

A second before the light changed to red, a green SUV was approaching the intersection, trying to catch the light. The driver observed Robert's car moving forward and pressed hard on his horn in hopes of forewarning Robert to stop before he was farther into the street. The driver knew he was driving too fast to stop in time and lost all hope. Robert looked up through the driver's side window and saw the bright headlights coming toward him and his life flashed before his eyes. All that he could see was Elise.

The two cars crashed, people stopped at every light at the sound and sight of impact. A Southern African American woman in her seventies, dressed in a tan gown with blue shoes and a white knitted overthrow, exited her car and approached Robert as fast as her body would allow. Five other concerned people, four men and one woman, left their cars to check on everyone involved in the accident. The five individuals split up to help in two directions. Another lady, still standing next to her car near the accident, called 911 and prayed for the safety of the ones involved. The initial car that was hit was a black sedan. The driver was also running late for work and attempted to make a left turn before the light turned red. When the black car was hit, it bounced toward Robert and the boy. Robert didn't brace his self for impact; instead, he climbed to the backseat as fast as could to cover the boy who was awakened. Miraculously, the car planted in front of them after it rolled over twice and landing on its top side. The front bumper of the green SUV was ripped off and had nothing left except the evidence of impact after its collision with the turning car.

Smoke streamed out of the green SUV's hood, creating a small cloud which led into the sky. The driver bled immensely as he sat still with no movement, except for the twitch in his hands. Two of the men that ran over to help had attempted to remove the man out of his truck but they were afraid to do so because they weren't sure of the man's condition. They called out looking for someone to help, but there was no answer. Robert heard the men but didn't help because he was gathering himself. *There's no way he's going to survive,* one of the men thought, shaking his head in disbelief. Robert was shaken and was still sitting in his car with a blank look on his face after being only a few feet away from where the two cars collided.

Robert turned around between the two front seats when the Southern woman had finally arrived to where Robert was.

"Are you OK?" She asked, concerned.

The boy woke up frightened, grabbing Robert tightly around the neck. Robert looked at the woman and replied in a panic-stricken voice, "Yeah, I'm fine."

"Is the child all right?" She asked.

"Yeah, he's just afraid."

The woman was relieved to hear they were OK. "You are a lucky man." The woman said in a serene voice.

"Oh, and how so? I was just in a car accident with a little boy in the backseat and he isn't even mine."

"Yes, but your car wasn't even touched. Where I'm from that's called a miracle."

"Well, where I'm from that's called dumb luck."

"Oh no, honey, I don't believe luck had anything to do with this miracle."

Robert became irritated. "I'm sorry ma'am, but I don't believe in miracles. At least not anymore."

A single tear rolled down the right side of Robert's face after he spoke. The woman had felt in her heart that something drastic happened in his life.

"Is everything OK?" She asked.

Robert looked down at the boy's seatbelt after having trouble unbuckling from the backseat.

"Here, let me." The woman offered.

"Thanks."

"You are more than welcome honey. I don't mind helping people out whenever the Lord allows me to."

"That's good." Robert said, wanting to stop the conversation.

"So what's the boy's name?" She asked.

Robert didn't reply to her right away. He was too distracted by the commotion around him. "I don't know." Robert paused as he saw the people struggling to help the man out of his green truck. "I have to help those people."

"You should probably worry about yourself and wait for the ambulance to arrive, I'm sure they'll be here shortly." The woman implied.

"You don't understand! I'm a paramedic and this was my shift. I'm supposed to be here. I have a responsibility to these people." He looked deeply into her eyes and the woman could feel the aching in his heart. "Can you please watch him?"

The woman nodded and grabbed ahold of the boy's hand, escorting him to the side of the street as Robert turned and raced toward the truck.

"Somebody help!" One woman screamed, being overwhelmed by ambiance of fear tending to the other involved party.

"Move aside!" Robert said to the men and then checked on the man inside the truck. He noticed the man wasn't breathing and pointed to the two men standing near. "I need you two to help me lift him out of the car."

The men did as they are asked and laid the man on the ice-cold asphalt. Robert kneeled, placing his ear over the man's mouth. He removed his blue work jacket and dropped it on the ground to gain full motion of his limbs. At that moment, he arranged his left hand over his right and placed them on the man's chest.

"One, two, three, four, five, six, seven, eight, nine, ten . . . ," Robert counted while pressing down on the man's chest, commencing CPR. Robert positioned his ear by the man's mouth again to see if he had started to breathe, but it seemed there was no life in him. Robert performed CPR two more times but still nothing. He shouted at the man, not wanting to quit on him, "Come on, come back!" Robert shakes his head, "Wake up!" He cried because he couldn't save him and looked at the rest of the helpers attempting to get the other driver out of his car.

"Where are the paramedics?" One of the men asked, and as soon as the words left his lips the car caught on fire. One of men from the group yells out, "Oh God!"

Robert immediately lifted his head after seeing the fire erupt abruptly. Three of the men grabbed the dented, partly open car door fearlessly and attempted to rip it open completely. Even with all their effort, the men were still unable to successfully pull the door open.

The man inside the car appeared to have passed out. He was leaning forward with his head tilted against the steering wheel and his arms were hanging down to the sides of his body.

Meanwhile, Robert had once again continued pressing on the man's chest in hopes to revive him. "One, two, three . . ." On three, the man inhaled like he had been holding his breath under water. Robert was exhausted, his breathing was abnormal but he asked a woman near if she could stay with him while he went to help another. She did so without hesitation and Robert ran to the other car to help.

The sirens from the ambulance and fire truck were heard by one of the men, "They're almost here." the man said out loud.

Robert arrived at the car where the man was trapped to help, but after one look, his eyes widened with a frightened expression. The firemen and the paramedics finally parked near the car, using the Jaws of Life to rip the door off the car. Robert took tiny steps away from the car after seeing the man. The paramedics readied the stretcher and placed the man on it so they could carry him to the ambulance. The fire was extinguished by the firemen and the Southern woman and Elise's son walk to the ambulance where Robert had went.

"Are you OK child?" The woman asked, but Robert stayed silent with his head dropped into the palm of his hand, leaning against the ambulance. "Honey, what's the matter?" The woman tried again but Robert closed his eyes trying not to cry, shaking his head to say he's fine. "Oh Lord!" the woman said after realizing something tragic had happened. The woman introduced herself as Mae Nell Harris to Robert, hoping he would feel a little more comfortable talking with her and then mentioned to him that he could talk to her if he'd like. Robert slowly stood to his feet and moved to the side, out of the paramedics' way. The paramedics wheeled the man to the ambulance and lifted the stretcher, placing the man inside the ambulance as Robert watched, standing there, sorrowful, and said in a faint voice, "Demetri!"

Chapter Four

Love Heals

1 Corinthians 13:4-7 (KJV)

*Charity suffereth long, and is kind; charity envieth not;
charity vaunteth not itself, is not puffed up, doth not
behave itself unseemly, seeketh not her own, is not easily
provoked, thinketh no evil; rejoiceth not in iniquity,
but rejoiceth in the truth; beareth all things, believeth
all things, hopeth all things, endureth all things.*

A continuous lengthy beep; the sound of a flat line is heard as the doctor and two nurses attend to the sound of death in the hospital. Demetri had cuts, bruises, and blood spotted on his clothing and his body. Nicole, Demetri's wife of three months, was being restrained by a nurse right outside of the surgery room doors; tears covering her cheeks.

"Jesus help! Please heal my husband so he can be healthy again, in Jesus's name!" She cried out.

A second female nurse who rushed into the room stopped and said to Nicole, "I understand how you may feel, but please, we need you to stay out of the room right now. Someone will come and update you soon." Nicole accepted the reality and said yes in a soft, scared voice. The nurse walked in and closed the door behind her as she entered the operating room. Nicole's head dropped and her eyes closed as she gripped her hands together up near her chest. She was standing in the hallway alone, still in front of the operating room doors, when she heard a man's deep, yet soothing voice speak.

"Everything will be fine." The voice said, but when Nicole looked up around hall there was no one there. She was surprised when she saw no one was near her. After the voice spoke, the only thing Nicole heard was the still silence in the air. "Thank You Jesus!" She said as her tears rolled down her cheeks.

Big Momma happened to arrive at the hospital after leaving the scene of the accident because she had a checkup with her doctor. She exited the elevator coming from the lower floor, saw Nicole crying and said, "Is everything all right child?"

Nicole heard Big Momma speak with her Southern accent and replied in a troubled voice, "Yes, ma'am."

Big Momma strolled closer to Nicole and said, "Well, where I'm from, crying with tears and without a smile doesn't generally mean that everything is all right." Big Momma paused, hoping for a response, but Nicole stayed quiet. "If you would like someone to talk too, then by all means, feel free to come and talk with me. I'll be over in the waiting room for a little while if you feel the need." On her way to the waiting room, Big Momma spoke, "The Lord said everything will be all right. Don't worry yourself and trust in Him."

Nicole watched as Big Momma entered the waiting room and slowly started to walk to her so they could talk. But as she took a step she heard an eerie voice in the distance, "You're going to be alone."

Nicole immediately stopped in her tracks and collapsed to her knees. Tears pounded the ground as she struggled to breathe, then a man came from behind and helped her to her feet. Nicole was shaken by the voice, and so she wrestled herself from the man, not wanting to stand. "Nicole, stand up please!" the man said in a deep quiet voice.

Nicole heard the man call her name but didn't recognize the voice fully. He sounded a little like Demetri, so she stood to her feet slowly with the man's help. He was so gentle when he was helping her off her knees that Nicole actually thought it was Demetri.

"Do I know you?" Nicole asked after she looked at the man.

"No, ma'am, I don't believe so. Why do you ask?" he said with a smile.

Nicole gazed at the man, trying to think where she saw him, but she couldn't remember where. She reflected on when the man said her name, "It's just that your voice sounds familiar to me."

"Oh, I don't believe we've met before," he said and then followed up with a question. "So what were you doing on the floor, if you don't mind saying."

Nicole thought quickly to herself, not really wanting to answer the question, but for some reason she felt comfortable enough to say, "My husband was in a car accident, and I have no idea what is going on with his condition. Then I heard a voice that was angelic say everything will be all right and that gave me hope. But then a whisper in my ear told me . . ."

Nicole nervously laughed, thinking about what she heard. The man asked what the voice said, but just the thought of it caused her to tear up. "The voice said that I would be alone. I just don't know what to do. I've never been this afraid in my life."

"You believe in God right?" He asked out of the blue.

"Yes, of course."

"Well then, don't be afraid and trust Him. I have seen many people get into a bad situation, and as soon as they find out that it's out of their hands, they tend to lose faith." The man implied, "What if your husband was in your place and you were in his, wouldn't you want him to stay hopeful and trust that God will fix it?"

Nicole wiped the tears from her eyes and nodded when she heard this man speak of Demetri as if he knew him.

"You're right" Nicole said.

"Yes, and I know a lot more than you might think. Your husband is a very wise man and he was chosen by God."

Nicole looked to her left and then back to the man, when out of nowhere he pointed down the hall to where a woman nurse was walking toward them. Nicole looked right to where the man was pointing and saw the nurse. She turned back toward the man and asked, "What?" But when she looked he was no longer there. Nicole looked around but thought to herself she might have been seeing things. The nurse was curious after she observed Nicole looking at a few of the doors.

"Excuse me, Mrs. Thomas?" the nursed asked curiously.

Nicole turned toward the woman with a perplexed look on her face. "Yes?" she answered while looking in all directions, still looking for the man.

"Is everything all right?" the nurse asked.

"Yeah, yeah. Everything is fine," she said with tears still building in her eyes.

"OK, well, we have an update to give you on your husband's status." Nicole's attention was captured and she shook her head OK. "He is stable, but he has fallen into a coma."

"Huh?" Nicole said frantically. "Do you have any idea of how long he'll be like that?" She asked, but wasn't sure if she wanted to know the answer.

"Well, Mrs. Thomas, these kinds of things we aren't too sure about. When someone slips into a coma, we can never predict when they will resuscitate to a conscious state. The best thing to do right now is to be patient and wait." Nicole recalled the voice that told her she would be alone and started believing it. She nodded but didn't say anything. "I'm sorry about the bad news, I wish there was more I could do." the nurse said right before she turned and walked away.

Nicole then entered the waiting room and walked to Big Momma before sitting in a chair.

"Hi," she said with a troubled voice. "Would you mind if I sat here?"

"No, go right ahead. It is a free country you know." Big Momma laughed silently causing her entire body vibrate. "Well, as free as it's going to get." Nicole smiled and took a seat. "Oooh, child, you have such a beautiful smile. I remember when I had a beautiful smile like that. I used to be a knockout." Nicole laughed lightly and the woman finished, "I ain't lyin', honey."

Nicole was enjoying the woman's company so she decided to introduce herself.

"I'm Nicole by the way," she said, wiping the rest of the tears from her face.

"I'm Mae Nell, Mae Nell Harris" The woman introduced herself. "It is very nice to meet such a lovely young woman with a heart of gold. You remind me a lot of my daughter Renee when she was your age."

Nicole's eyebrows rose by a hint of curiosity. "What do you mean a heart of gold?"

"Well, I know when I see the joy of Lord and it's in you. His joy is what helps us to smile through such hard times."

"So what is your story?"

"My story?" Big Momma asked.

"How come you're here at the hospital?"

"Oh, I'm just here for a checkup with my doctor."

"A checkup for what? You seem perfectly fine to me." Nicole said in a cheerful voice.

"Well, about thirty years ago, when I was forty-two years old, I was diagnosed with type 2 diabetes. I was new to the idea of having diabetes and didn't know exactly what to do. But after a few years of having diabetes, I went to see a doctor and he prescribed me insulin. The thought of having diabetes was scary at first, but I did what the Lord and my doctor told me and I took the insulin that was provided."

"How long were you afraid?"

"Nearly every day for some months, but because I know a God who can do all things the fear slowly began to fade."

"How were you able to become so strong? Wasn't it hard?" Nicole asked.

"Well, it definitely wasn't easy that's for sure." Mae Nell paused to think about how far God had brought her and then continued, "You know Nicole, just because we get placed in the wilderness, it does not mean that God has left us there alone. The Lord said in Hebrews 13:5, that he will never leave us nor forsake us."

Nicole thought to herself, *Is God with me?*

"Nicole, the wilderness you're in, with your husband being in the hospital, is only temporary. Sometimes God will place you somewhere to make you stronger and I believe this is your wilderness. But don't let it fool you. The wilderness is not to bury us down deep under the dirt, but for us to prepare for what challenges may come before us."

Nicole looked at Mae Nell with a look of distress in her eyes as she continued.

"Whatever it is that has torn you apart inside, you must let it go and let God repair you, because through Him it is already done."

Big Momma spoke in such a nice and compassionate voice that caused tears to steadily flow slowly from Nicole's eyes and cheeks. Her head sank low as she leaned over on Big Momma's shoulder.

"Oh, child, don't fret yourself. Everything will be fine, I just know it!"

Nicole was still crying and she clenched both of her hands together in a fist, and held them up near her heart. "I need help, I can't do this alone." Nicole said. Nicole's voice faded in and out as she spoke. "Mae Nell . . . I heard a voice telling me that I was going to be alone. Almost immediately after, I heard another voice say everything will be fine. I don't know what to believe, and it doesn't help that I can't see anything farther than what is in front of me."

Mae Nell rubbed Nicole's head gently to calm her down while saying, "And that is why you must give it all to God, because His love can heal you and He can fix everything you ask Him to fix."

Six hours earlier, Nicole was at home with Demetri watching a movie and waiting for dinner to finish heating up. There were only five minutes left on the oven timer and Demetri was sitting on the couch watching television.

"Dinner is ready" Nicole said when the time went off.

"OK I'll be right there." Demetri said, but before he got up, he remembered the food was still hot. Nicole looked at Demetri and he was glued to the TV. "Don't wait too long or your food will get cold" Demetri laughed and Nicole smiled and then, in a curious voice, asked, "What is so funny?"

"My mom use to tell me that all the time."

"Oh yeah, and what else did she say?"

"Nothing!" Demetri whispered.

"Nothing huh?"

"Yeah, nothing, she wouldn't say anything, but if I didn't come I was getting popped in the head."

Nicole laughed and said, "Well, if you don't want me to pop you on your head, then I suggest you come have dinner with me."

"Well, if you hit anything like my momma, then it looks like I'm on my way."

"You are just too much," she said wholeheartedly.

Demetri walked over to their kitchen table. The table is pure oak wood with four rounded legs. It has a chair on each of the four sides, and all the chairs have red cushions on them except for the one closest to the kitchen. Reason being is because the dining set was a gift from Demetri's mom and when he moved out the house he lost it during the move. When he walked next to the table he stood to the side of it, looking at the spread Nicole had begun to set before him.

"Man oh man, how lucky does a man have to be. I have beautiful, caring, and loving wife like you, and you can cook! If God ain't good then I don't know who is."

Nicole laughed at Demetri's silliness and said, "Just sit down."

After he sat down he picked up his drink to get a little taste.

"You have to say your prayer first baby" Nicole states.

"I knew I was forgetting something," Demetri joked. "Your prayer," he said, trying to get a laugh.

Nicole gave him a funny look and said, "OK, OK. Now you need to pray."

After she sat in the chair across from Demetri, he then began to pray. "Lord we first want to thank You for this wonderful day. We thank you for bringing us together for dinner once again as husband and wife. Lord we thank you for blessing us with this food that we are about to receive. May it bring nourishment to our bodies and may you remove all sickness from us and give health. In Jesus's name we pray, Amen!"

Nicole looked at Demetri with a smile on her face as he immediately started to eat, and then she said, "I love you!"

Demetri looked up with spaghetti sauce around his mouth. "Huh?"

Nicole giggled. "I said I love you!"

Demetri smiled and said "I love you too!" There was a short silence in the room for a few seconds before Demetri spoke. "Where did that come from?"

"I was just thinking how good God has been to us by keeping us together and happy."

Demetri smiled, and replies while trying to chew his food, "Yeah, He has been good to us, hasn't He?"

The two of them locked eyes and smiled, then after looking at her watch Nicole said, "You better finish your food before work. You wouldn't want to be saving people on an empty stomach."

Minutes later, Demetri finished his food and he left the table to get ready for work. When walking into his room, Demetri saw his clothes were already ironed and laid out across the bed, prepped to put on. He changed out of his gray sweatpants into his navy blue work pants and placed his short sleeved navy blue button-up over his white T-shirt. Then he sat on his bed and put on his black high-top boots and laced them up. He then noticed he was not wearing his necklace with a cross as the charm. After tying his shoes, he walked to the dresser and reached to a small drawer which he pulled open to get his necklace. He picked it up and held it out in front of his face while looking in the mirror.

"Lord, please watch over me as I'm working, in Jesus's name I pray," Demetri said after placing the necklace around his neck.

Nicole came up behind Demetri, hugged him around his neck and then kissed him on the cheek. "Is everything all right?" she asked after seeing a troubled look on his face.

"Yeah, I'm fine," he replied with a sad glare in his eye

Nicole slid in front of Demetri, grabbing his left hand. She leaned closer and her right hand extended gently toward his face. She wiped a tear from his cheek that had crept out of his tear duct slowly.

"Baby!" she said in a loving voice. "God is watching over you, and I'm not the only one who will wipe away your tears."

Demetri smirked as he blinked. Nicole reached her arms around Demetri's body, hugging him as tight as she could.

"I love you!" she whispered in his ear.

"I love you too and thank you for always staying by my side."

"I'll always be by your side. Remember, until death do us part?" Nicole said with a bright smile until she saw the time on the digital clock sitting next to the small drawer the necklace was lying in.

"Looks like it's time for you to get to work, love. I don't want you to be late." Nicole kissed him on the lips and said, "I'll see you later"

"Not if I see you first," he responded and smiled as he made his way toward the door. When he walked outside of the house and entered his car, Nicole was standing by the frame of the door leaning against it. Demetri looked over and blew a kiss, and when Nicole saw him do so she reached her hand out to catch it, then placed it on her lips. Demetri smiled and left for work.

Three minutes from the intersection where the accident occurred, Demetri was pondering about the dream that Joseph had told him about the day before. *I'm looking forward to hearing the meaning of that dream,* Demetri thought. He looked to the left side of the street as he was approaching the intersection and saw his brother Daniel. Demetri was in disbelief, shaking his head and continued driving after believing he was seeing things. He looked up at the traffic light up ahead and it was still green, so he decided to speed up to be sure the he could make the light. Almost to the light, it turned yellow as Demetri was approaching the intersection. He thought to himself *I have to make this light.* When Demetri entered the intersection and began to make the left turn onto the main street, a green truck ran the red light but never noticed Demetri making his turn. The two of them collided in the middle of the intersection, but seconds before the crash Demetri looked to his side, and saw a car with an exuberant golden glow surrounding the interior of it. His car flipped twice and slid across the ground.

There's no way that person could have survived, a woman nearby who witnessed the accident thought. People from different directions got out of their cars and raced across the street to do all they could to help. The ambulance and the fire truck finally arrived and cleared everyone away from the accident. Robert was frozen solid seeing Demetri inside the smashed car and was asked by the firemen to move aside so they could pry the car open.

"Why Lord?" Robert cried out and then paused, shaking his head in question to God, *Why is this happening to me? First this little boy comes and invades my life and now this. Demetri is leaning close to death's door and I can't help but feel it's my fault. So tell me why!* Robert thought angrily at God. *What have I done to have so many things in my life go wrong? Elise left again and I can't do anything about it.*

At this point, Robert was disgusted with his life and walked over to one of the ambulances. He leaned against the side of it and said loudly, "God if you're really there, do something. I've never seen anything that was a result of a miracle, so do me a favor if you want me to believe. Show me anything that I can believe in, because I have nothing that's worth believing in anymore."

After speaking those words, Big Momma and the boy walked next to him. Robert was looking at the ground, but he glanced over and saw the boy and whispered, "Malcolm."

Big Momma looked at Robert, confused, and asked, "Excuse me?"

"Malcolm, the boy's name is Malcolm." Robert told Big Momma because that was his own father's name, but he was still unsure of the boy's name.

Big Momma knew the truth without him saying, but she ignored the fact Robert didn't know the child's name.

"Honey, I was thinking that it would be a good idea if you didn't go to work after being involved in an accident."

"I'll be fine." Robert said, emotionless.

"You should really think about what you do next. You have this handsome young man to look after now, and he needs you."

"Not for too long. I already have enough problems of my own and I don't need any extra, especially if it's not mine."

"That's where you're wrong." Robert developed a confused look on his face. "Everything happens because God allows it to happen, and only because you need it."

"A little boy that I don't need, and Demetri in a bad condition. That sounds exactly like someone who just lets things happen. If you ask me, God looks from above and doesn't care what we go through." Robert said in a high tempered voice.

"Robert, whatever it was that happened in your life that has made you angry toward God, you must let it go and give it to Him. God will take care of the pain and heal every fiber of your being if you allow Him to." With every word Big Momma spoke, her tone never changed, and because of that Robert began to wonder why she was so kind.

"Look ma'am, I don't mean to be rude, I just don't have any faith in God to do anything for me anymore. And it's all because of moments like earlier. I've seen way too many bad things happen daily in this world to trust God. Putting my faith in someone who won't take their time to save someone isn't going to happen."

"I'm sorry to hear that, but you have to know that God has always been there, even when it doesn't seem like it. Yes, I know that a lot of horrible things happen daily in this life, but that isn't God's fault."

"But you said yourself that He allows these things to happen."

"Yes, but that is because He loves us enough to give us free will. If God was to control every action and decision you make in life, it just wouldn't be worth living now wouldn't it?"

"I guess, but I'll live how I've been living these past few years, thanks anyway."

"I'll be praying for you, young man. People care for you. You just have to open your heart so you can see."

Robert felt the love of God radiating from Big Momma and was overwhelmed. "Goodbye Mae Nell." Robert said as he picked up the little boy and carried him to the car. Big Momma stood still watching Robert carry the boy away over his shoulder. The boy looked at Big Momma and gave her the cutest smile she had seen recently.

"Lord, please help that young man. He needs You now more than ever." Big Momma said.

One of the paramedics pulling the stretcher with Demetri on it asked Big Momma kindly to move aside. Big Momma nodded and watched as Demetri was lying on the stretcher, and began to pray.

"Lord I've been in this life for so long and I've never came across all this. One man is very hurt and another is angry at you because of something that has happened in his life. I've said what I did and I've done all I can, but now Robert needs you to come in his life and take a stand. This young man who is hurt, I have no idea who he is. But I see the pain on his face and I really pray that he gets through this.

Lord, carry them through this life, protect them from harm. Their storm is just beginning so I pray all the bad You help them. In Jesus's name I pray. Amen!"

After carrying the boy whom he called Malcolm to the car, Robert placed him in the backseat. He buckled the boy's seatbelt and to his surprise, the little boy's eyes were wide open and staring right at him.

"So you're Robert? The boy asked knowingly.

"Yes, I'm a friend of your mom's. She asked me to take you to your great grandmother's house while she was at work. Now I just have to give her a call back and let her know I'm on the way."

The boy looked Robert up and down and then looked at the ground before shaking his head no.

"Why are you shaking your head no?" Robert asked. "What you don't want to go to your great grandma's house?"

The boy, still looking down, says, "But my mommy doesn't work."

After hearing that bit of information, Robert became curious about who the boy's father is and how Elise takes care of him.

"So where is your dad?" Robert asked, but he wasn't sure himself if the boy had a clue.

The boy said nothing; instead, he shrugged his shoulders.

"Well, I'm going to take you back to my house to eat, and then I'll call your grandma and let her know we're on the way. The boy told Robert OK and after that Robert shut the car door. Once he opened the driver's door he paused. Robert looked back at Big Momma as she drove away and wondered, *Where did she come from?*

Chapter Five

As I Lay to Rest

Isaiah 29:8 (KJV)

*It shall be as a hungry man dreameth, and behold, he eateth;
but he awaketh, and his soul is empty: or as when a thirsty
man dreameth, and behold, he drinketh; but he awaketh,
and behold, he is faint, and his soul hath appetite: so shall the
multitude of all nations be, that fight against mount Zion.*

October 20, 2004

Joseph woke abruptly from his sleep, sweating and breathing rapidly, clutching the bed sheets and trying to catch his breath. The doctor, who was standing across the room holding a clipboard, rushed over to check on him.

"Are you OK?" The doctor asked.

Joseph nodded his head and took a deep breath and replied, "Yeah, I'm fine, it was only just a dream."

"That must have been some dream for you to wake up like that." The doctor said sarcastically. "By the way, I'm Dr. Trust. I will be your doctor for the rest of your stay here." Joseph chuckled to himself and Dr. Trust smiled, knowing why Joseph was laughing. "Yeah, I know it's a very different name, but I can assure you that I can be trusted."

Joseph shook his head side to side with a grin on his face. "And I bet you say that to all the girls?"

Dr. Trust smiled. "Actually, I used that line only once and the woman laughed at me so bad, and right in my face."

"Oh yeah, and then what happened?"

"Well, we ended up dating, and then four years later, we were married."

"Where is she now?"

"Sadly, my wife, she passed away a few years ago from breast cancer."

"I'm sorry to hear that."

"Thank you, but there's no need to be sorry. It would have taken a miracle to heal her."

"What was her name?"

"Her name was Laila." Dr. Trust smiled halfway. "She was the last person on this earth that could keep me going when this job tried to get to me."

"What do you do now?"

"I simply think of something she would say."

"My grandma always said that we should always try and keep our good memories because those are the ones that will help us to smile in time of need."

"Your grandmother is a very wise woman."

"Yea, she was."

"All right, well enough about me. Do you have any questions about your health?"

"Well, Doc, honestly, I haven't asked any questions because I know there isn't anything wrong with me. My God has taken care of me all these years, so I know he'll continue to do so."

"Oh, a man of faith I see."

"Of course," Joseph said proudly. "What better way to go through life than to trust a God who can do all things?"

"I'm glad to hear you have some hope. Most people that come in here are so worried about what could happen to them that they forget about what can't. I never understood it."

"So do you go to church around here?" Joseph asked.

Dr. Trust looked at the clipboard and clenched his hands tightly on the sides of the clipboard.

"No, I don't go to church anymore," he stated. "I don't feel that I need to be in church just to connect with God."

"I hear you, but I used to think like that too until I figured out that going to church is not just to connect with God alone, but to join in fellowship amongst the other saints of the church in Christ. But regardless whether you're in church or not, if your relationship with God isn't right, you'll still never know what you might do when you're with people who live in the world."

Dr. Trust heard him, but wasn't particular to hearing about God. "Thanks," he responded.

"No problem."

"So would you at least like to know when you'll be leaving from here?"

Joseph laughed, almost forgetting where he was. "Yeah, actually, I would."

"OK so . . ." Dr. Trust paused shortly. "After seeing the results from the first x-ray, I wanted to take another look just to be on the safe side."

"Was there something wrong?" Joseph asked.

"Well . . ." Dr. Trust looked down at the clipboard and then back at Joseph. "It seems as though you have developed a rather large tumor in your brain."

Joseph was in disbelief. "If you're saying I have a tumor, I don't want my wife to know yet. She'll worry too much over it and she doesn't need that."

"Joseph, with all due respect I have to let her know."

"Doc, please . . . ," Joseph said calmly. "Just do this one thing for me. God has already told me everything is going to be all right."

"God told you?" Dr. Trust questioned with a grin. "How exactly did He tell you?"

"You remember when I woke up from that dream? Well, that's when."

Dr. Trust didn't comprehend what he was saying, thinking Joseph was still high on the medicine he gave him. "Doc, hear me out. This dream was so vivid and I didn't know exactly what it meant until now. But this is why I don't lean unto my own understanding, because the dream wouldn't make sense at all."

"So this dream is why you don't want me to tell your wife? I don't know if I can do that. No matter what you may think you have heard from God, I have to tell someone just in case something was to happen to you. Plus, what if your wife decides to ask me what your health is like? I can't lie, so what am I supposed to tell her?" Dr. Trust said intensely. "I just don't want to be held accountable for something this serious."

"I understand that silence is deadly, but just tell her that I said, I cannot see but I trust."

Dr. Trust stopped, wondering where he had heard that saying before. He looked at Joseph, pulled in his lips and shook his head, "I know I'm going to regret this, but OK. I won't say anything to her." Dr. Trust pondered on the phrase, "I cannot see but I trust." before the silence was broken. "If this is what you want then OK, but I can't promise you that I can keep it quiet for long, at least not from her."

"Thanks, Doc!"

Moments before Joseph woke from his sleep, he was having a dream like nothing he has ever had before.

Joseph was standing in a room made of a thick glass, built like an aquarium. Next to him was a woman with long straight black hair; her eyes were almost like hazel but with a bluish tint. He described her skin to be smooth, without a trace of a blemish. There was a light shining through the water in the next room to where he was standing. This light caused her skin to become radiant to where it appeared as a diamond with the sun shining onto it.

The woman and Joseph were standing next to each other and she began to slowly turn to him.

"Joseph," The woman said. Joseph closed his eyes briefly and the woman continued. "You have to finish."

Joseph's eyes widened and he was unsure of what the woman was speaking of.

"What do I have to finish?" He asked.

The woman looked at him and he saw a glare of expectancy in her eyes. She saw in his heart that he was slowly becoming the man God intended for him to be.

"Oh, Joseph, every task that is set in front of you, you will complete them, but you mustn't ever give up."

At that moment, Joseph looked through the glass and saw a giant blue whale; not blue like the sea but a grayish-blue. The whale swam around slowly and as Joseph continued to watch the whale, he said to the woman, "How can I move this?"

The woman pointed above the whale to where a balcony was sitting near the top of the ceiling, which was at the highest point of the water.

"Good luck, son," the woman said. But as quick as she spoke, Joseph looked to her, and she was no longer there. Instead, there was a hole in the ground where the woman was standing, which led to the water. Joseph walked over to the hole and stared into the water to see nothing, except the water resting beneath him. He inhaled and held his breath as he entered the water. Once inside the water he began to look around, and noticed that besides his movement swimming through the water, no one would ever know it was water which he was swimming in. Joseph's eyes became filled with amazement because the water is so clear, it's was as if there was nothing around him at all.

He then looked up and saw the whale swimming around in circles through the water. After remembering that he saw a man standing on the balcony above, he began to swim up toward him. He swam up, coming to the point where he had to pass the whale, and when doing so he gazed at the whale, reaching his hand out to touch it. While brushing his hand against the whale he noticed it was surprisingly smooth, not scaly like he expected, more like a dolphin's skin.

Out of his peripherals he saw the man standing still and proceeded toward him. Once he arrived at the peak of the water, he stuck his head out and wiped the water over his head, away from his eyes. When Joseph arrived on the balcony across from the man, he was stunned at what he saw and began to stare at him. The man looked like a white shadow, except he was standing instead of lying on the ground. He had no appearance; except if you looked close enough, you were able to see the features of his face.

Because Joseph wasn't able to make out who the man was from his face, he asked him, "Excuse me sir, do I know you?" The man didn't speak. He just continued to look down into the water at the whale. "Why is the whale inside such a small area?" The man still said nothing. Instead, he lifted his hand and pointed his index finger toward the water. "What is it?" Joseph asked.

The man with the emotionless face finally spoke, "You must set the whale free so that it can be seen by all the fish in the sea."

"What do you mean? And how am I supposed to set the whale free?"

The man pulled back the hand which he was using to point and spread his fingers. Joseph watched and saw a tiny seed. The man looked at his own hand and stretched it out toward Joseph. "Take this seed and use it. How you will use it will come to you when you choose to do so."

Joseph had a look of trust in his eyes as he took the seed from his hand. After obtaining the seed, Joseph looked at it and thought to himself, *What am I going to do with a seed.* "Why won't you tell me what to do?"

"Just because you don't see now, does not mean you won't see when it's time." Joseph thought of the seed in his hand and clenched his hand tight, securing the seed. "You must complete what you have been putting off."

And the man had finished, but Joseph was clueless as to what the man was talking about, because his mind was focused solely on setting the whale free. With that thought, he dove into the water, swimming down until he was near the whale. *This gentle giant swims around so peacefully,* Joseph thought until he wondered if he should even set the whale free since it seemed comfortable being there. When he looked around under the water, he saw a brick wall and began to swim to it.

Once arriving at the wall, Joseph remembered he had the seed in his hand and thought, *Maybe I'm supposed to leave the seed here until it grows large enough to knock the wall down.* But after this thought, he knew that it wasn't right. *If the seed was to grow under water, I would be waiting for a while.* But then Joseph noticed his movement was a lot more fluent. He seemed to move faster than when he was swimming to the balcony. Joseph tried everything he thought possible to break down the wall but nothing worked. All he seemed to do with all the punching, the kicking and the pushing was making himself tired. After thinking intensely of what to do, Joseph swam away from the brick wall, only about twenty feet away, and waited there. He took the seed in his right hand and reached behind his head, ready to throw. Joseph thought to himself, *I hope this works,* and he lunged his arm forward and released the seed toward the wall. The seed moved swiftly through the water, and it even picked up speed the farther it went, until it was a foot away from the wall. It slowed down, and the hopeful expression that had built on Joseph's face suddenly dropped. But the speed didn't take away all of his faith. He was still a little hopeful that something would happen when the seed made contact, but his hope began to slowly decrease as he watched.

By the time the seed reached an inch away from the wall, it appeared to not be moving at all, so Joseph began to swim to try something else. But as soon as he neared the seed, it touched the wall and all of the mortar between the brick began to crumble. Joseph watched as the brick shattered into pieces as if it was made of glass. Joseph was shocked, not only from what happened to the wall, but because of the soft impact causing such destruction. The pieces from the wall scattered on the floor of the water and slowly descended piece by piece.

Joseph swam back to the whale and was instantly captured by the magnificence of it. Then he decided to stop on the side of it, looking directly into one of its eyes. He saw himself in the reflection of the whale's eye, but in his reflection, he was wearing all white attire. Joseph realized it and he looked at his clothes, but he was wearing nothing like what he saw in his reflection. While he was wondering what was going on, the whale swam toward the opening Joseph created with the seed. While the whale swam through the opening Joseph heard the woman's voice from earlier say, "I'm proud of you son!"

Joseph looked around for the voice and then . . .

Joseph woke up in the hospital, springing upright and gasping for air. When he was breathing properly, he and Dr. Trust conversed until the doctor exited the room. Five minutes before Dr. Trust left the room, Joseph's wife, Sarah, arrived in the parking lot of the hospital with tears in her eyes. Before exiting her car, she wiped the tears away from her eyes, and then she walked to the hospital. When she entered the hospital Sarah went to the front desk clerk and said, "Excuse me miss, I'm here to see my husband and I wanted to know if he was still in the same room."

"What is the patient's name?" The clerk asked.

"It's Joseph Johnson. He was upstairs in room number 137 the last time I was here."

"OK just one second." The clerk said as she entered Joseph's name into the computer. "OK I found him . . . and it looks like he's in the same room."

"Thank you for your help." Sarah said and proceeded to the elevator. Before arriving at the elevator, she crossed paths with a woman who was walking toward the hospital exit. The woman stopped after taking a glance at Sarah.

"Excuse me, is everything all right honey? You're looking a little down," she said.

"I'm fine." Sarah said while wiping her face to make sure there were no tears left. "Everything will be fine by the grace of God."

The woman smiled and said, "Amen! By His stripes we are healed."

Sarah looked up at the woman wondering if she knew her husband since they were in the same hospital. "Do you know my husband, Joseph?" *That couldn't be possible*, she thought after she asked the question.

"No, honey, the only Josephs I know are the ones I read about in the Bible." The woman chuckled to herself and said, "Your husband will be fine. You're already doing the right thing by speaking life into the situation."

Sarah paused for a few seconds. "What do you mean?"

"Well, speaking life comes down to faith, speaking those things that are not as though they were. God spoke the universe and all of its inhabitants into existence. For example He said, 'Let there be light' and there was. Because we are the children of God we inherit the same gift to speak things into existence if we believe. People hear that the power of life and death is in the tongue, but some don't know that what you speak are things hoped for and not seen."

The elevator reached the bottom floor. The doors opened and Sarah asked, "So what do I do?"

"Just keep doing what you've been doing and know the Lord is going to make everything all right."

Sarah smiled, showing her pearly white teeth and said, "Thank you. What did you say your name was again?"

"My name is Mae Nell Harris, but you can call me Mae Nell."

"Nice to meet you. I'm Sarah."

"It's nice to meet you as well."

"So Mae Nell, if I ever need to reach you how could I get in touch with you?"

"I'll be around, just look for me here at the hospital. But if you ever need to talk immediately you could call this number." The elevator door closed and Big Momma said, "Sarah, it looks like you just missed the elevator."

"It's OK I'll just get on the next one."

"All right, well, remember to keep your faith in God."

"I will, I will." Sarah said.

The other elevator door to the left opened and a man and a woman walked out holding hands. Sarah saw them and noticed their hands are locked. She smiled, and in her eyes was a shimmer of hope that was perceptible after her eyes caught the two hands tightly held together.

"Keep smiling child, not just because you have a beautiful one." Big Momma told Sarah and finished with, "Now don't you miss this elevator, I'll be seeing you around" Big Momma said with a big hearted voice.

Sarah says OK and then she slipped in to the empty elevator.

Big Momma proceeded to the front of the hospital where she was met by her daughter and my mother, Renee and my brother Isaiah and I. Isaiah was sixteen at this time and I was twelve.

"Hey, Grandma!" I greeted her with an immense smile.

"Oh, Michael get over here and give your grandmother a hug."

I walked over to her and wrapped my arms as best I could around her.

"Hey, Grandma, how are you?" Isaiah asked. He was the quietest between us two and our oldest brother, but he loved talking to Big Momma when he got a chance.

"I'm blessed Isaiah, I haven't seen you two in so long. The two of you have gotten so big." Big Momma looked around and asked my mom. "Where is Shawn?"

"Shawn won't be here until tomorrow. He had to work late and he didn't want to miss out on the extra money before the holidays. But he did say he'll be on the train first thing in the morning."

"Oh, that's all right. All that matters is the entire family is together." Big Momma grinned. "So what do you want to do today?"

I jumped up excitedly and held my tummy. "We're going to eat, grandma! I'm hungry."

"Well, let's get out of this boring old place and go get some food."

When we walked to the car, Isaiah and I were in front of our mom and Big Momma so they could keep an eye on us. But on our way to the car my mom started to think about Big Momma's health.

"Mother, don't you think you should be at home resting? You just got through taking those tests."

"No, Renee, I'll be fine. It was just a checkup, and plus, God never said I couldn't spend time with my family."

"I just don't want you to be exhausted dealing with these boys. You know how they can get."

"They aren't that bad. You just don't let my sickness get you all worried and stress yourself out. God has everything in control, and when it's my time, it's my time. So I'm going to do the things I love to do until I know I can't do them anymore."

"OK, but if you start feeling sick let me know, OK?"

"I will, but like I said, don't you be worrying about me."

"I won't."

"Where's your car at anyways?" Big Momma asked.

"It's at the house." She told. "I figured since you live so close we could get some exercise and ride with you back to the house."

After my mom helped Big Momma into the car she entered on the driver's side.

"Boys, make sure you're buckled up." My mom said and then started the car. She looked over at Big Momma before driving off and smiled.

Back inside the hospital, Sarah had just exited the elevator and saw Dr. Trust writing on his clipboard behind the check-in desk on the second floor of the hospital.

"Excuse me, Dr. Trust?" Sarah asked.

"Yes, that's me, what can I do for you?"

"I'm Sarah Johnson, Joseph Johnson's wife. I just wanted to get an update on his condition before I go in and see him. I'm sure he's probably talked your head off by now."

Dr. Trust laughed a little, knowing why she would say that. "Oh, I know exactly who you're talking about. But regardless of how much he may talk, he still seems like a great man."

Sarah smiled emphatically and said, "Yes, he is."

Dr. Trust flipped the pages on the clipboard until he reached Joseph's page. "Well, it looks like . . ." Dr. Trust paused while looking down at the paper and back up to Sarah after thinking of how he could keep Joseph's attention from her. "Mrs. Johnson, I'm sorry but your husband has asked me not to tell you if anything is wrong with him. He asked that it be doctor and patient confidential."

Sarah eyebrows rose and her eyes widened after hearing the surprising news.

"I know how this sounds and have an idea of how you may feel right now, but he did ask me to tell you, 'I cannot see but I trust.'"

Sarah looked down briefly and asked, "Can't you tell me something? I would really like to know what is going on with him. I mean, for him to have just passed out for a few of hours, he should've been released home by now."

"Mrs. Johnson, I understand, but if your husband doesn't want to tell you it might be for a good reason."

But Sarah shook her head, still not understanding why Dr. Trust and Joseph wouldn't let her know what was going on. Her eyes began to water as she became more fearful of what might have happened. Dr. Trust could see the hurt and pain in Sarah's eyes as she cried and felt that he should tell her, but because he told Joseph he wouldn't, he kept his word.

I now see why your husband didn't want me to tell you anything except, 'I cannot see but I trust.' Dr. Trust thought before speaking. "Maybe you should go see your husband. I think it would be better if you asked him yourself and see how he is doing."

Sarah agreed but didn't say another word. She couldn't help but be worried over what she might find out about Joseph's condition.

As Sarah walked to Joseph's room, Dr. Trust added, "Mrs. Johnson, I believe if your husband is putting all his trust in God, it might be wise if the two of us did the same."

Sarah nodded instead of saying OK and then turned and walked to Joseph's room. Dr. Trust on the other hand thought, *God I'm having a hard time with this because of what happened to my brother all those years ago. But for me to see what I saw in that man's x-ray, You must be real and doing something in that man's life.*

Chapter Six

Protection from Above

Psalm 91:11 (KJV)

*For he shall give his angels charge over
thee, to keep thee in all thy ways.*

A fter a long day at work, Dr. Trust pulled up in front of his home. He exited his truck and walked to the front door of his house, while pulling his keys out of his front left pocket. After obtaining his keys, he rambled through them until he got ahold of his house key. He reached and unlocked the door and began thinking about what Joseph said, "I cannot see but I trust." For some reason he wasn't able get the phrase off his mind.

Finally unlocking the front door, he entered and looked at the floor after almost slipping on his mail. He picked up the mail and sorted through it, but then came across a letter addressed to his younger brother with no sender name or a return address. Dr. Trust walked farther into his house after shutting the door behind him and setting his keys on the kitchen counter. He loosened the tie from around his neck, allowing it to hang loose while trying to decide on what to do with the letter. His nerves began to build up the longer he looked at the letter causing him to sweat, so he unbuttoned the first couple of buttons on his white long sleeved dress shirt. Dr. Trust clenched his eyes, pulled in his lips, and let the letter slide out of the palm of his hand, opening his eyes to watch it as it floated to the ground.

"Why are you doing this to me?" Dr. Trust yelled at God. "Why is this letter coming after all these years? My brother has been dead for years now, and then out of nowhere this letter comes for him." Dr. Trust paced back and forth and came to a stop. He was so furious with God that he looked up and pointed to the roof while he yelled even louder. "You know you have some sense of humor God! Doing this to me. I don't find this funny one bit!" He paused very shortly looking for the words to say. "You know there isn't a day that goes by that I don't think of what happened, and now I seem to be being tortured to see his name. Oh, and to top it all off, I'm here looking like a fool, practically talking to myself and receiving no response from You. You know what God? Some friend you are. You don't even help me forget about something that has caused me so much pain. And why won't You speak to me! Don't you see I need You?"

Dr. Trust was furious toward God and had hurt himself more with all the bickering. Then he decided to walk to the refrigerator and get some wine, hoping it would ease the pain. He downed one bottle after another while sitting in a chair until he became sleepy. He went upstairs to his room, but mistimed the third step from the top and tumbled down the stairs. When he reached the last step, he bumped his head hard and he immediately saw a white light shining to the left of him, coming from around the corner in the kitchen. He thought the fridge was left open, but wasn't sure after the head injury. Slowly inching off the ground, Dr. Trust started to walk toward the light he saw, but the more he walked to the light the farther away it got.

After seeing the light push away, he decided to stop pursuing it. He gave up and turned away to walk back to the stairs so he could try going up again. When he reached the stairs, he started climbing but his legs became heavier with every step he took as if there were cement blocks surrounding his feet. He attempted to take another step, but this time his feet were cemented to the ground. He pushed and struggled with all his might, but he was still unable to lift either of his legs. As he continued to struggle, his legs finally started loosening a little, when suddenly both legs were free of the weight. Dr. Trust fell back to the bottom of the stairs after losing his balance once again. But this time he stood to his feet, holding his head while pursuing to the top of the stairs which seemed to be a challenge. From the kitchen, he heard someone singing. So he turned and stepped down the stairs and the voice became more projected. The voice was coming from the kitchen where the light was shining, which had him become curious to see. When he reached the light, he stared into it and saw his brother inside the light walking with him down the street. It was a vision or some sort of memory he had, because he remembered that day.

"CJ." Dr. Trust whispered, but there was no answer, until he heard the sound of a gunshot go off. He saw two men running toward him when his brother called his name.

"Anthony." CJ said. Dr. Trust responded but he found out shortly that CJ wasn't talking to him, but that didn't stop him from trying to get his attention.

"CJ, run!" Dr. Trust yelled, hoping to get his attention, but his effort was in vain. Dr. Trust ran to the light right next to his brother, but CJ couldn't see or hear him. The two guys running toward Dr. Trust both pulled out guns and started shooting. Dr. Trust saw the guns and immediately ducked behind his kitchen counter. When he heard the first gunshot, he heard himself call CJ. Dr. Trust peeked around the counter to see him and his brother running to get out the line of fire, but then he tripped. CJ felt Dr. Trust fall beside him, so he stopped to help his older brother up, but when he did a gun went off and . . .

Dr. Trust jerked awake in the front seat of his car after waking up from his nightmare. He looked around and saw that he had never left the hospital parking lot. He woke up because his phone rang. The sudden stir quickly brought him to reality, causing him to wipe down on his face to loosen up the tense muscles. Dr. Trust picked up his phone and looked at the caller ID and saw it was the hospital calling. He answered immediately, with his speech being lightly affected since he barely woke up.

"Hello." He answered.

"Dr. Trust! We need you to come in immediately." The hospital desk clerk alarmed him.

"I'm on my way." He responded and then asked. "How long have I been gone?"

"You've been gone for three hours. Sorry for the page, but we need you here right now.

"It's fine, what's the emergency?" Dr. Trust asked the clerk to fill him in on what was happening while he got himself together.

"It's one of your patients. He looked to be having different patterns and movements on his face. No one knows what is wrong with him and we thought maybe you knew something we didn't."

"Which patient is it?"

"It's Demetri Thomas"

Dr. Trust was looking down at the floor of his car, but when he heard Demetri's name, he lifted his head instantly and he said, "I'm on my way!"

Dr. Trust hung up the phone and hurried out of his car and went to the hospital elevator. As he was coming closer, he saw it was going up, so he decided to take the stairs. Only three flights of stairs from the underground parking garage and he was there. Dr. Trust was jogging up the stairs but then started running, since he believed the situation was urgent. When he reached the top of the stairs, he walked through the entrance door and looked right, but went left, deciding to sprint until he arrived at Demetri's room.

With all the running and dodging people in the way, he finally arrived and entered the room where he walked to the immediate side of the bed.

"Demetri!" He called out in a soft voice. "Can you hear me?" There was no answer, but the look on Demetri's face at the time was immeasurable; at least that's what Dr. Trust thought. "Demetri if you can hear me then I need you to move your right hand."

There was no movement except for the measure of countenance in Demetri's face, and Dr. Trust had no idea himself what was happening to him.

"Dammit!" Dr. Trust said as the seconds on the clock passed by until there was no pain on Demetri's face. *What is happening with you?* Dr. Trust thought while thinking of no possibilities. Whatever was happening to him, Demetri appeared to be back to normal, and Dr. Trust decided to walk out of the room into the hall and lean his forehead against it.

The elevator opened as soon as Dr. Trust leaned against the wall and he heard the ding coming from the elevator doors. As it opened, he looked over and saw Demetri's wife, Nicole, exiting. Nicole noticed

Dr. Trust was standing across from Demetri's room and said, "Dr. Trust, how is he doing?"

Dr. Trust looked at her, unsure. "He's doing fine now."

"What do you mean now?" She asked.

"A few minutes ago, I didn't know what was happening to him. I received a call from the hospital, so I hurried up the stairs and saw Demetri's face. It appeared he was having a nightmare for only a few seconds when I arrived, but then out of nowhere it all stopped." Dr. Trust felt helpless for the first time since his brother passed. Nicole became worried, but you wouldn't know it unless you concentrated on her eyes.

"Is it OK if I go and see him?" She asked.

"Yeah, go right in. I'll be right here in the hall for a little while longer if you need me."

"Ok." Nicole said and then walked into the room.

Without hesitation, Nicole pulled a chair over to the right side of Demetri's bed. She sat in the chair and dragged it right up to the bed until there was no room between her and him. She grabbed ahold of his left hand and looked directly at the wedding ring the hospital staff left on his finger.

While looking at Demetri, Nicole began to tear up. "I'm holding on baby." She said. "So don't you worry about me, OK? I know you're watching me and know it has been hard these past couple of days, but God has given me all the strength I need to carry on." Nicole paused briefly to hold herself together. "Baby, I just came here to check on you and to let you know that everything at home is going great." More tears began to fall down her face while she stood to her feet slowly and reached her hand out to brush against Demetri's cheek. "Demetri . . ." She paused again, but this time only for a few seconds longer than before to gather her composure. "You're going to be a father." Nicole continued to shed tears, but wiped away each droplet as they fell from her cheek. "I know you'll be awake to see the birth of our first child. I know you wouldn't miss it for the world." Nicole leaned over and gave Joseph a kiss on his forehead and said, "I love you!" After the kiss, Nicole stood upright and gazed at Demetri for a few seconds before praying. "Lord I don't know what's going on with him, but I need Demetri back. I need him as soon as possible if not now, in Jesus's name I pray, Amen."

Nicole walked to the door quietly and then stopped to take one last look before she left. "I'll be back tomorrow as soon as I can, OK?

Nicole then left the room and saw Dr. Trust was now sitting in a chair with his elbows on his knees and his hands upon his head.

"Dr. Trust, are you OK?" Nicole asked.

There was no answer so she asked again.

"Is—"

Dr. Trust lifted his head, cutting Nicole off to try and make it seem as if he was all right. "Yeah . . . Everything is fine."

"Are you sure? You seem like something is bothering you."

"No . . . Nothing at all. I'm doing fine, just thinking what to do next."

"Well, what are your choices?" Nicole asked in a quizzical manner.

That's what I'm trying to figure out. Dr. Trust thought. But because he didn't know how to respond, he quickly changed the subject. "You shouldn't come by too often. You wouldn't want to wear yourself out emotionally. I've seen many loved ones of coma victims almost lose themselves because they are always so certain that they'll wake up soon. But the reality is, comas aren't predictable, no matter whom you have on your side."

Nicole grew a little uneasy after the heartless remark from Dr. Trust, so she went to the elevator and didn't say anything back. The elevator dings after opening and Nicole entered to leave.

"God can help you, you know." Nicole said as the elevator doors shut. Anthony lifted his head and stood sluggishly with the thought of checking on Joseph.

At the time the nurse had called Dr. Trust, there was a man walking down the street. Five blocks over from where he was walking, there were two young boys walking the street as well; one of them was eight and the other was thirteen. The two boys were heading home after leaving the park where they were playing basketball with their friends.

"How much longer Julian?" The eight-year-old Sam asked his thirteen-year-old big brother.

"We only have a few blocks to walk until we're home."

"Good, because I'm hungry and I want to go play some video games."

"Is that all you do, play video games? I hardly ever see you doing anything else."

"You play video games too." Sam whined.

"Yeah, but nowhere near as much as you do. Most of my time I'm playing basketball so that one day I can go to the NBA."

The two boys were silent for a little while after that, and they saw three kids throwing a football to one another, two blocks down the street.

"Do you really think you can make it Julian?" Sam asked out of the blue.

"What are you talking about?"

"Do you think you'll play in the NBA?"

"Yes, of course. I'm going to be like Michael Jordan."

Sam giggled. "You aren't going to be that good."

Julian stopped walking and said, "Yes, I will, just watch. I'm going to be the biggest basketball star ever. And when I do, I'm going to buy a huge house and have a basketball court instead of a swimming pool."

"Why not just have both?" Sam asked curiously as they started to walk again.

"Because I don't like to swim all the time, and plus, I'll be too busy playing basketball and training to get better."

"Why don't you just get a basketball court on one side of your backyard, and next to it you can have a swimming pool? That way you can always play."

Julian smiled at his younger brother and asked, "You just want to swim don't you?"

"I just thought I could swim and you can play ball at the same time. That way you won't have to be mad when you have to bring me along everywhere."

"I don't get mad because I don't want you around. I just don't want to get in trouble if something happens to you. You and I both know that mom blames me for everything that goes wrong with the two of us."

The boys were a little farther down the street and Julian stopped again. "Sam, hold on we'll cross the street right here."

Sam stood next to Julian and they readied themselves to cross the street. The boys looked both ways and Julian said, "We'll cross after the next car." When that car finally passed, Julian said, "OK, let's go." The two of them stepped off the curb on the street and start walking across.

"So why do you want to swim all the time Sam?"

"Because I'm a fish and I love the water, and it's the most fun thing in the world."

When the boys were halfway across the street, a car was driving down the street, speeding. The driver saw the two boys ahead of time, but didn't think of slowing down since they would be across by the time he arrived.

The three kids who were throwing the football were having a great time, until one of them threw the ball too high for either of the other two to catch. The ball went over the head of both of the kids and bounced into the middle of the street. Julian and Sam were stepping up the curb on the same side of the street as the boys when Sam said, "I got it."

At that moment, the sun was shining right inside the driver's car, almost blinding him, and Sam was running to get the ball for the kids.

Julian then ran into the street himself, after seeing the car coming and yelled, "Sam, look out!"

The driver was holding his hand up in front of his face to block the sun, so he didn't see Sam kneeling down in the street to recover the ball. The driver had believed he saw something cross the street but was unsure. Sam turned his head and saw the car and a frightened look fell upon his face. The driver slammed on his breaks and turned his wheel hard left to avoid hitting whatever he saw was running into the street. The car slid toward Sam.

"Sam!" Julian screamed, hoping to get to him in time.

Julian barely reached Sam, just seconds before the car's impact and pushed him as hard as he could out of the way. But unfortunately he failed to avoid the car himself. Sam went flying to the side of the street while Julian fell to his knees, clenching his eyes tight and covering his head with his arms. The three boys that were throwing the football all had a scared look on their faces. The driver looked through the front passenger's window, seeing Julian at the last minute and shouted, "Jesus!" In a split second, the car made contact, hitting the middle of passenger's side of the vehicle. The two tires on the driver's side lifted inches off the ground before landing. When Sam landed, he was lying on his back, with his elbows holding him off the ground after being pushed, and saw a blinding light between the car and his brother.

Sam's tears started to dry on his face and he softly whispered, "Julian."

Julian was breathing fast after the shock of the car coming toward him and answered, "Yeah?"

"You're OK, don't worry."

Julian was shocked as he opened his eyes and slowly looked around.

"You were saved by somebody."

Julian looked around, but he only saw the car that crashed and the man who was inside. "What are you talking about?"

Julian then stood to his feet and looked around once more, but he still wasn't able to see anyone except for the man and the three kids that threw the ball. The man was frightened after thinking he had hit a child. He wiped the sweat from his forehead with his left hand and sat in the car for about twenty seconds before exiting his vehicle. When he finally slowly exited the car, the man was holding the back of his neck, but still hurried over to where he saw the boys standing, afraid that they were hurt.

"Are you OK?" he asked.

"Yeah, we are." Julian replied as Sam nodded his head. The man glanced shortly at his car and saw a huge dent on the door and began to wonder what he had hit if wasn't the boy.

"Are you boys sure you're OK? I thought I hit one of you," he said, confused.

"No, we're fine. Don't worry about it." Julian told the man.

He looked at the boys and placed his right hand on top of his head, wondering, *how could this be? The two boys were in the way but were saved.* "So where were the two of you headed?" he asked the boys politely.

"We're on our way home." Julian said, deciding to keep it short since they didn't know him.

"I could give you a ride if you'd like?"

"No, that's OK, but thanks. We're almost home anyway."

The man could see that Julian didn't want his help, but he gave them a few hundred dollars from his wallet. "I'm sorry I almost hit the two of you. I know this won't do anything, but it's the least I can do." After he handed the money to Julian, he decided to estimate the damage cost and the boys made their way home once again.

"I can't believe that happened." Julian thought aloud.

"I saw a man Julian." Sam confessed.

"What are you talking about?"

"Well, first I saw a bright light, but when the light was going away, I saw a man with wings."

"You were seeing things Sam."

"Nuh-uh. I really did see him. He covered you when he stood up, like he was a blanket."

Julian started to become irritated with Sam's insistence talking about seeing a man. "Sam there wasn't a man, quit saying that."

"But I did see a man, I really did."

This time Julian ignored him because he didn't want to hear any more.

"So you didn't see him did you?" Sam asked in a disappointed voice.

"No, I didn't." Julian could see that Sam really wanted to believe in the invisible man so he played along. "It was probably because my eyes were closed."

Sam's eyes and smile amplified. "So you believe me?"

"Yeah, I believe you." Julian said after thinking Sam probably wouldn't have made something like that up for the fun of it.

"Do you think it was an angel?"

"Could be."

"Ooh, do you think we'll see him again?"

"If it was an angel, then yeah, we will, but probably not until we go to heaven."

"Yeah, but that would be cool if the angel came to say hi, don't you think?"

Julian smiled a little and said, "Yeah, actually it would."

When Julian looked up, he saw that they were only a few houses away from being home and the street lights were getting ready to come on, so they walked a little faster while talking.

"Hey Sam."

"Hey Julian." Sam replied, joking around.

"You aren't going to tell mom about what happened, right?"

"No, I won't."

"OK good, because the last thing I need is for mom to be on my case."

"I don't think she would because you saved me."

"Well, I do. She'll come up with something, somehow."

After Julian and Sam finally made it home, there was a man standing near the accident, watching the driver as he looked toward heaven. Back at the hospital, as Nicole was leaving the room, a single tear rolled down the side of Demetri's face until it could no more.

Chapter Seven

You Must Trust, Even When You Don't Think You Can

Proverbs 3:3-7 (KJV)

Let not mercy and truth forsake thee: bind them about thy neck; write them upon the table of thine heart: So shalt thou find favor and good understanding in the sight of God and man. Trust in the Lord with all thine heart; and lean not unto thine own understanding. In all thy ways acknowledge him, and he shall direct thy paths. Be not wise in thine own eyes: fear the Lord, and depart from evil.

October 21, 2004

"I'm sorry Robert. I can't take on a child in my old age. Also, it's not my place to do so." Elise's grandmother, Mrs. Robinson responded.

Robert was unsatisfied with her response so he explained further, "You don't understand. There is no way that I'll be able to take care of this child either. For one he's not mine; two, I have a full time job; and three, I wouldn't even know where to begin. I don't even know that boy's name nor do I have any idea of how to take care of a child."

"Robert, I really wish I could help, I really do, but like I already said, I'm not well enough to take on the responsibility of a child. You're going to have to find some way to do this without me until Elise shows up."

"There has to be something you can do?"

Mrs. Robinson felt bad that she couldn't take care of the boy so she offered to help the only way she was able to. "I'll tell you what, I can see if I can get in touch with Elise."

Robert became frustrated as he wondered how he would be able to take care of the boy until his mom returned. But even though he was upset, he was still grateful at Mrs. Robinson for helping him. "Well, if or when you do get in touch with her, please give me a call as soon as you can."

"I will Robert. You just stay strong and trust God. There has to be some reason why you were chosen to take care of him. God will never allow a situation to happen and not help you."

Robert shook his head, not caring about what God would do. "Thank you Mrs. Robinson," he said sincerely.

"You're welcome Robert and God bless. Oh, and there's something you need to know." Robert's attention was captured as he waited shortly in anticipation for the words that follow. "His name is Malcolm"

Robert was surprised to hear that name, but he just smiled and politely said, "OK, thank you. Thanks a lot."

"I thought it would be helpful for you to know."

"What made her name him Malcolm?" Robert asked curiously.

"When you talk to her you should ask. She will be able to explain it a lot better than I can . . . and besides, it's not my place."

"OK, well, goodbye, Mrs. Robinson."

The two of them hanged up the phone, while Robert shook his head in disbelief, looking at little Malcolm.

Forty minutes earlier, Robert and Malcolm arrived at his house and Robert thought, *What am I going to do with you?* Then while looking at Malcolm he asked, "So what's your name?"

Malcolm only stared at Robert with no response. He lifted his right arm and pointed his index finger seemingly in-between Robert's eyes, who was only standing a few feet away.

Robert laughed hysterically but didn't know why he did. "What's with the pointing?" he asked kindly.

"I know you." Malcolm said perceptively.

Robert became confused, but he still smiled when he asked, "Is that right?"

"Yeah, she talks a lot about you and she couldn't wait to come see you, because she said it's been a really long time."

Robert's emotions then shifted dramatically as his face dropped flat. He looked at Malcolm and said, "I'm sorry about the other day with your mom. You might not understand what's going on because it's complicated, but you should know that I'm sorry."

Malcolm looked at Robert and nodded, and at that moment, Robert thought, *Where is your mother at?* Malcolm could see Robert was confused and walked right in front of him, looking up at his face. When he saw Malcolm looking into his eyes he smirked. Malcolm smiled back and wrapped his arms tightly around one of Robert's legs, holding him tight and not letting go. Robert smiled emphatically because of the overwhelming sensation of happiness that he hadn't felt since he was with Elise. He reached down and lifted Malcolm off the ground, holding him tight while a single tear gently rolled down his face. Robert then flashed back to the first time he remembered feeling that joy—when he was with Elise.

Seven years ago, when Robert was eighteen and Elise was seventeen, they were in their senior year of high school and were part of the 1997 graduating class. They had never been boyfriend and girlfriend, but they have been in love with each other ever since the day they first met. On that day, Robert was riding his brand new chrome bike, which he had received from his dad in 1990 on a beautiful Christmas morning. Before he received the bike, his dad had been teaching him how to ride with an older bike, so he had intermediate experience riding the bike. But that didn't stop him from deciding to ride up to the highest hill in Barstow, California. Once he arrived at the top of the hill, he looked down and paused until he gained his composure. He took a deep breath, inhaling to his max, and then releasing calmly, placing his feet on both pedals and gripping the handlebars to prepare for the adrenaline that would be pumping through his body.

"Lord, keep me from harm, in Jesus's name, Amen!" Back then, Robert was a lot closer to God and he prayed before everything he did, especially if it was dangerous like this day. He prayed before he made his way down the hill, just in case. When he finally took off, racing to the bottom with the cool air blowing in his face, he was filled with excitement. It wasn't until he neared the bottom of the hill that Robert's heart began pumping. As he approached the end of the hill, he came to a slowing stop after and wanted to do it again. But unfortunately, after accomplishing what he had wanted to do for so long, Robert had to head back home because there was only an hour left until the streetlights came on. While he was riding as fast as he could he thought, *If only I could do tricks like the pros, then I'd have it all.*

When Robert arrived four houses away from his own, the sunlight was almost gone. Seeing he was only a few houses away he figured he had time to attempt a wheelie. He pulled on the handlebars while leaning back at the same time, and did his first wheelie. It only took him a few tries until he felt he had mastered the art and he could do it higher and longer. Then Robert looked over and saw some of the neighborhood kids playing tag with their new scooters so he decided to show them his trick.

When he reached the area where the kids were he called out to them, "Hey guys!"

The attention of the eight kids was grabbed at the sound of his voice and they all stopped playing to listen to Robert.

"Watch what I can do!" Robert said excited to show them he could wheelie.

He pedaled about ten feet away from the kids and stopped. One of the boys in the group said, "Hurry up, we haven't got all day."

Robert inhaled and exhaled deeply, ignoring the words of the boy, and started pedaling just fast enough to roll forward while on his back wheel. When he pulled the handlebars and leaned back to perform a wheelie, the kids were amazed. That is until he leaned too hard and fell backward along with the bike. Robert looked up in pain as the neighborhood kids laughed at him. One of the kids even called him a loser as they all walked away. He tried to hide his face because he was embarrassed, until he noticed not all the kids were laughing at him. There was one young girl who walked over and asked, "Are you OK?"

"Yes." he replied as she helped him off the ground.

"Are you sure? You fell pretty hard."

"Yeah, I am. I'm tough." Robert said confidently.

The girl giggled because Robert was trying to act all macho.

"What's so funny?" Robert asked.

"I'm just laughing because you're a typical boy. Never wanting to show emotion in front of a girl."

"I'm not being typical. This is just me being me."

Robert leaned over to get his bicycle. The girl saw that he was struggling to pick up his bike so she offered to help, but he said he wanted to do it on his own. She watched as he lifted his bike off the ground and then introduced herself.

"I'm Ashley by the way."

"I'm Robert," he said while checking if his bike was good to ride down the street to his house.

"You know, sometimes it's good to have help." Ashley said.

"I know but I'm better doing things on my own."

"Ashley, it's time to come in!" A voiced interrupted from a distance.

Robert looked to see where the voice was coming from and he saw it was an older girl around his age. He curiously asked, "Who is that?"

"Who is who?"

"Who is that calling you? She is the prettiest girl I've ever seen!" Robert said dramatically.

"That's my sister Elise. Would you want to meet her?"

That's what he wanted most of anything at that moment, but he was too nervous to approach her. "Uh . . . I don't know I should. I have to be home soon."

"Well, you don't live far. I've seen you around here before and besides, it won't take that long."

"Yeah, I live three houses down the street."

"That's two houses over from us."

"Yeah. But my dad and I are new around here and he would probably want me home."

Ashley looked at Robert in disbelief. "Stop making excuses. You've been here for two weeks already, and your dad came to the neighborhood welcome barbecue that you didn't show up to. I heard him talking all about you to my mom, and she wanted you to meet my sister anyway. I don't know why, you don't seem that special to me."

"Well, I know whom to come to if I ever needed to know something around here."

"Ashley, come on! You said you were going to help dye my hair." Elise interrupted.

"I'm on my way, and I have someone who wants to meet you." Robert's heart began racing as the nervousness jolted through his chest. "Robert you don't have be nervous, she's just a girl." Ashley giggled.

"I'm not nervous!" He said after gulping.

"Well then, come on!" Ashley grabbed ahold of Robert's hand and dragged him over to meet Elise.

"Do you think she'll like me?"

"We're both about to find out. Just don't act like you did with me after you fell."

"I didn't fall!" Robert defended himself.

"Yeah, and you don't have a crush on my sister either."

When they arrived at the front door of the girl's house, Elise was waiting to see the person that wanted to meet her since she didn't recognize him.

"Elise, this is Robert." Ashley said.

Elise reached her hand out to greet Robert and said, "It's nice to meet you."

"Hey Elise!" Ashley interrupted "Do you remember the firemen who mom was talking to at the barbecue? Well, this is his son."

"Oh yeah, I've heard a lot about you." Elise stated.

Robert grinned, hoping it wasn't anything bad. He knew how his dad could get when he talked about him.

"What did he say?"

"Oh, I don't know. You'd have to talk to our mom."

"Maybe next time." he replied with a smile.

"But your dad did say it would a good idea for us to meet since all the kids in the neighborhood are five years younger than us."

"What about your sister?"

"She's a little thing as well."

Robert and Elise continued to laugh and giggle while Ashley ignored them. Instead, she smiled because she was excited to have united a potential perfect couple.

"Looks like I've done my job." Ashley said.

And that very moment is what created this special friendship that eventually formed a love between the two. Although not many people who are seasoned in the love experience would call what they had true love, the two of them didn't think of what anyone else would say.

"It's a shame that we're going to be graduating high school in less than a month. I'm going to miss everyone!" Elise said sincerely as she leaned to Robert's shoulder.

Robert was sitting to the right of her on the couch and responded almost right away. "Yeah, I know what you mean. It's going to be so much different without seeing everyone."

"I just can't believe how popular you became in school. When you first started school, not many people seemed to like you." Elise said sarcastically.

"I wasn't a loser. I was just the new kid in town."

"Yeah. But you did have some loser characteristics, and you carried them throughout your entire high school career." Robert remained silent, just to take in the warm inviting sound of her voice. "Aren't you going to say anything?"

Robert shook his head and reached his arm around her shoulders. She smiled and gave Robert a soft peck on the cheek after feeling sheltered lying in his arms.

"What was that for?" Robert asked.

Elise smiled and said, "Just cause."

Robert was overwhelmed with joy for the simple fact that he has always wanted Elise to kiss him, even if it was just a peck on the cheek.

"I have something I want to tell you, but I'm just not sure how or if I should."

"Just tell me, you know you can tell me anything no matter how silly it may be."

Robert chuckled because what he was about to tell her was nowhere near a joke.

"I'm not going to lie, I'm a little scared."

"You're scared? You mean to tell me the fearless warrior Robert Brown is afraid of something so small like a conversation?"

"Well, it's not so much of the conversation. It's more of what the outcome could be."

Elise turned to face him, looking deeply into his eyes. "I love you!"

Robert's eyebrows rose and his eyes widened, causing his forehead to wrinkle up. For a second he felt his heart stop completely after hearing those tasteful words flow from Elise's lips. At first he didn't even know what to say except for, "Huh?"

Elise giggled seeing he was stunned and kissed him on the lips and then smiling after. "I said I love you, silly!"

Robert was once again overwhelmed with joy, but this time he tried not to show any feelings too much.

"Really?" he asked, unsure.

"Yes, really! I wouldn't have said it if I didn't mean it."

"I don't know what to say." He said with a smile. "You kind of stole my thunder." He pulled Elise closer just to give her the biggest hug possible and whispered, "I love you too! I've loved you since the first second I saw you standing on your porch."

"I remember that day." Elise said reminiscing. "That was the day you told me that I was beautiful just the way I am. And if it wasn't for you, I wouldn't have my red hair anymore."

"I can't believe you were going to dye your hair black. That would have been so plain."

"Did you really mean it when you said it would take away from my beauty? Because you know those kind of words mean a lot to any woman."

"Of course I did. You know when I speak it's never almost the truth. But If I could go back to that day I would go ahead and let you dye your hair so you could see how silly you would look."

"I could always go do it right now you know?"

Robert developed a big grin on his face, "No, you wouldn't. But please don't, because I wouldn't want you to be anything other than how God created you."

The two of them enjoyed a smile with one another until the room was completely silent.

"Robert?" Elise said softly, breaking the silence.

"Yeah, what is it?"

"I want to ask you something, and can you promise that you'll tell me why?"

"Yeah, of course." Robert became eager to hear the question, even though he was afraid at the same time, knowing what the question might lead too.

Elise breathed in and out and gazed deeply into Robert's eyes.

"How come you never told me this before?" he asked.

"What, that I love you?"

"Yeah! I'm sure you had to know that I loved you as well."

"Because . . . I was afraid," Robert answered, knowing what was about to follow and he pulled his arm back to himself, creating a shell around his body and heart.

"What was there to be afraid of?" Elise asked.

"It's not that at all. It's . . . it's a lot more complicated than you think."

"It can't be that complicated. Does it have something to do with your mom and dad?" He didn't respond so she asked again, "Robert, can you please answer me?"

Robert knew he was able to trust Elise and he sadly said, "It has everything to do with my mom and dad." Robert continued as Elise looked at him with concern. "Mainly because my mom died when I was young, and I've always been afraid that it could happen to me. The one thing I fear most in life besides God is being in love, and then being alone and not having a family or any friends to care for me, or me for them."

Elise reconnected with Robert, grabbing ahold of his hands and then brushing her hand across his cheek.

"You don't need to worry about that because I'm not going anywhere, anytime soon." Elise looked deeper into his eyes, gripping his hands a little tighter. "I promise!"

Robert looked up at Elise and was able to feel what it was like to trust someone, other than his dad, for the first time in his life

"I want to tell you something else that's very important to me."

Elise became very curious and asked, "What is it?"

Robert took a deep breath and says, "It's about my mother."

Elise was shocked because Robert has never talked about his mom, even after all these years. But for some reason, he chose to share.

"The year before me and my dad moved here, we were living in Henderson, Nevada, with my mom. Even at a young age, I could see that the two of them were happily married. My mom was the one who had an actual working job as an elementary school teacher, whereas my dad was one of the best musicians I've ever known before becoming a fireman. When it happened, I didn't know what was going on. All I know is I was at home drawing cartoon characters when my dad walked through the door holding his head down. When I saw my dad I grabbed my drawing and ran to show him. He looked bad. His shirt was halfway off and torn, and his glasses had cracks on one side. My dad only took two steps through the door before I saw my mom's necklace that he had given her for their ten year anniversary slip from his fingers."

"Is that the one that you wear around your neck?" Elise asked interrupting the story.

Robert pulled the necklace, around his neck, from out of his shirt and looked at the cross charm, with a line from a poem his dad wrote to his mom engraved on the back: *I knew it was really you when I felt your love that day. When we touched our hands together just so we could pray.*

"Yeah, this is it." Robert continued. "This is the only thing that I have to remember my mom by. My dad gave it to me at her funeral and I haven't taken it off since. But at that moment, when I saw my dad drop my mother's necklace, I fell to my knees in tears, trying to cry out to God, except, I didn't know what to say to God since I wasn't sure what happened. The feeling in my gut had me turned upside down though, so I knew it was bad. It took me three whole weeks to finally build up enough courage to finally ask my dad where mommy was. But even then I wasn't sure if I wanted to know. I wanted him to tell me she had gone to visit family or she hadn't come home because she was mad at my dad or even me for something one of us did. All I know is I didn't want her to be gone forever."

Tears that Robert hadn't shed since that day began to release from his eyes while he struggled to continue. "When I went to my dad I asked him, "What happened to Mom?" I will never forget the way my dad looked at me. I knew he didn't want to break my heart, but he knew that I needed to know.

He looked me in my eyes and said, "Your mom is . . ."

"Robert, are you OK?" Elise asked as Robert started to choke up from telling the story, but wanted to continue.

"Yea . . . Yeah, I'm fine. It's just hard to think about this, nonetheless talk about it."

"You don't have to tell me you know."

"Yeah, I know, but I want too." Robert asserted as he looked Elise sincerely in her eyes. Elise nodded and listened as Robert told the rest of the story. "My dad told me, 'Son, your mom is gone and she won't be back.' In the middle of that sentence he immediately burst into tears. I saw that and the next question I asked, I wasn't sure if I should have. The only reason I did was because I had to know." Elise wiped the tears from Robert's face and grabbed his hand tighter as he continued. "The next question was the last one I ever asked my dad about my mom. 'How did she die?' When my dad told me how, I wished I hadn't asked. The pain was a pain I've never felt in my life and I prayed that I never felt that again. 'Your mom was hit by a bus, head on in front of the school.'"

"How did that did happen?" Elise asked.

"Apparently a bus driver was under the influence and lost control of the bus. The bus dove in to the other lane and my mom must not have seen it in enough time to react and turn." Robert paused and thought to himself before saying, "But even though my mom's life was taken, all of those little children on the bus survived. Five of them had minor injuries and the driver ended up in critical condition and was hospitalized. For the longest time I hated him with a passion, but then with the help of God and my dad I was able to finally forgive."

"I don't see how you were able to forgive him. I don't think I would be able to unless God took my free will from me to do so Himself."

"It wasn't easy, trust me. It took a long while to become this forgiving person I am, and even with all the years that have passed, I still succumb to the pain of the memories."

"What happened to the bus driver?"

Robert's tears started to dry up as he spoke. "The last thing I knew, he was in prison rotting for life because of involuntary manslaughter and driving under the influence—and what's worse, children were in the bus with him. I used to be happy that he was alive to feel some of the same pain I felt from what he did, but other times I feel sorry for him."

"Why would you feel sorry for him?" Elise interrupted.

"Because I know he's sorry for what happened?"

"How could you know that?"

Well, because me and my dad received a letter from him about two years ago, apologizing for what he did. Everything he said in the letter really meant a lot to me. But the one thing he said in the letter that stuck with me was, 'If God can find it in His heart to forgive me then I pray that you find it in yours to do the same.' I believe God used that letter as the rock-hard foundation to help me forgive."

Elise was grasped by the story, never hearing anything like it. The worst thing that ever happened to her was losing her dog.

"So this is why you became this guy who doesn't share his feelings all the time?"

"Yeah, that pretty much sums it up." Robert replied.

"Thank you!" Elise said.

"For what exactly?" Robert asked, confused.

"For giving me another piece of your heart. I know it wasn't easy telling me that."

The two of them locked eyes and began smiling.

"Close your eyes." Robert said.

When she did Robert reached to the back of his neck, unhooking the necklace and then placed it around Elise's.

When she came to realize what he did she said, "No, Robert! I can't, it's your mom's."

Robert looked at her sincerely and said, "It's yours now!"

"I don't think I can. I can't"

"Please! The engraving is the same from me to you as it was from my dad to my mom."

Elise was still unsure if she should take the necklace. It was more than a gift to be given to someone since it once belonged to his mom.

"But it's the last thing you have to remember your mom."

"Yeah, and we'll always be together."

"But what if something happens? What if you don't love me anymore?"

"Elise Aniela Magnano, I will love you always and forever."

Elise began crying tears of happiness and reached tightly around Robert. "Forever and always I will love you Robert Alexander Brown."

Chapter Eight

Your Faith Must Stand Trial!

James 1:3-4 (KJV)

Knowing this, that the trying of your faith worketh patience. But let patience have her perfect work, that ye may be perfect and entire, wanting nothing.

October 28, 2004

"Hey Joseph, how are we doing today?" Dr. Trust asked as he walked into the room.

"Well, I don't know about you Doc, but I'm blessed!" Joseph exclaimed.

"Oh, I'm doing mighty fine myself . . . So how's your head feeling?"

"Feels great, how's yours?" Joseph said while gripping his own head. Dr. Trust couldn't help but laugh at the ridiculousness of Joseph as he continued. "I knew you'd like that one, but I'm feeling great, Doc. Honestly, I don't feel any different from before I ended up in this bed, having to seeing you every day."

"That's a good sign."

"So what's going on today, Doc?"

"Well, first things first, I need to take you down to x-ray to see about that tumor."

"What are you talking about?" Joseph said acting as if he didn't hear about it, confusing Dr. Trust.

"Joseph, surely you remember the x-ray that I showed you revealed a fully developed tumor sitting on the right side of your brain?"

"I cannot see, but I trust. Remember? Just because you can't see now doesn't mean you won't . . ." Joseph continued as Dr. Trust tried to comprehend how he's able to trust so easily. "Be anxious for nothing, but in everything by prayer and supplication with thanksgiving let your requests be made known to God. And the peace of God that surpasses all understanding will guard your hearts and your minds in Christ Jesus."

When hearing the scripture, Dr. Trust placed his hand over his mouth, once again shaking his head in question.

"Joseph, how can you lay here quoting scriptures from the Bible, when you have seen the same tumor that I have?"

"Do you know what the scripture means?"

"Yes, but that doesn't matter right now. You need to get out of that Bible and get into reality."

Joseph, to Dr. Trust's surprise, wasn't moved by his words at all.

"Don't worry, just pray and let God, so that He may give you peace in your thoughts and your heart as you trust in Jesus." Dr. Trust looked at him tangled, not knowing what to think. "That's what the scripture is saying. Just trust God, Doc." Joseph whispered with tranquil in his voice. He could see that Dr. Trust's lack of faith in God was not helping the situation so he decided to level with him. "Look Doc, I don't expect you to understand or trust the way that God has helped me to. But you have to know that what God has shown me is true, whether you believe it or not."

"Joseph, you have to realize that the dream you had was just a dream and nothing more. Whatever you saw in your dream and what you have explained it to yourself to be doesn't mean a thing. I do believe that if we trust God, He will perform miracles, but your condition is fatal and there's no way around or through death. It just is."

"Like Jesus said to His disciples: 'Ye of little faith.' The idea of faith is to trust without knowing or seeing, and believe fully that Jesus Christ will be faithful to complete a good work in you. If I give in to what you're telling me, my actions are saying that I don't trust God to heal me."

Dr. Trust nodded with his lips tucked in and then said, "I'll be back."

Joseph looked confused, but didn't say anything to him. He just watched as Dr. Trust entered the hall and reached in to his pocket, pulling out his phone. The phone rang and a woman answered on the other end.

"Hello?" she answered.

"Hi, Sarah Johnson, this is Dr. Anthony Trust."

"Hi, Doctor, is everything OK?"

"I just wanted to talk with you about your husband Joseph. Do you have the time?"

"Yeah, what's going on? Is he behaving?"

"Yes, he is. It's just that he had asked me not to say anything if something was wrong with him, but I have to let you know the kind of risk he is taking." Sarah was worried now, wondering what went wrong as Dr. Trust continued, "Your husband has developed a very large tumor covering the entire right side of his brain."

Sarah was in disbelief shaking her head. "No . . . No, that can't be right, you have to check again."

"Mrs. Johnson, I understand how you may feel right now, but what I saw in the x-rays wasn't good. Joseph continued to insist that I don't say or do anything because he believes that if we just wait it out and trust God, then he will be fine."

Sarah heard him speak and understood, but she stuck by her husband's side, not knowing how she would be able to trust God for healing after hearing the news.

"Well, Dr. Trust, with all due respect to your profession, I'm going to have to go with my husband on this one. If he says to trust God, then trust God I will. Every decision he has made has always turned out for the good, and because I trust my husband with my life, I trust him with his own."

Dr. Trust was frustrated, hearing about trusting God. He wanted to perform the removal surgery but he wasn't able to get either of their consent.

"How can the two of you sit back and just watch him die. That tumor is massive and must have been there for some time. In reality, there is no way that he should be alive right now. The fact that he is still alive is a mira—" Anthony paused not wanting to say what he was about to. "Look there's just no way it's . . ."

"What, that it's a miracle?" Sarah cuts him off having heard enough of him speaking. "Well, this is exactly what it is." Sarah said barely believing herself. "God has his hands on my husband's life and it's time you start believing it. If you're going throughout life like this I know it is hurting you physically and mentally. Let God give you peace in your thoughts and in your heart." Dr. Trust never replied after Sarah spoke. He just sat there quiet still not wanting to understand. "Bye Doctor!" Sarah said calmly and a little frustrated, then hung up the phone. As soon as she hung up the phone, she broke down in tears and her phone slipped through her hand, hitting the hardwood floor in her store and cracking the screen.

Over in Demetri's room, his wife Nicole had just arrived to visit. She sat in a chair and began to speak. "Hey, baby, I'm back." She said happily, smiling at Demetri and stroking his hair. "I know it's only been a couple of days, but I've been thinking so much about our baby. I just want you to know that if the baby is a boy then we will name him after you, but if the baby is a girl then I want to name her Kelly Michelle, after yours and my mom." Nicole paused briefly, wondering why she was talking to him when he wasn't responding.

"Demetri," Nicole called out. "Baby, can you hear me?" She asked, hoping to hear his voice at least once, but there was nothing. "I don't know if you can hear me or not, but I need you to know that I'm trying my absolute best right now to live without you. I'm so used to you being here that I've been waking up and I start cooking for two as if you're coming home from a late shift. I even thought I felt you place your hand on my shoulder one night when I was crying. It really felt as if you were there with me, but when I opened my eyes you weren't." Nicole then moved, sitting on the side of the bed to be closer to Demetri, anticipating tears to flow from her eyes. "Baby, I've been angry at myself since you've been here. I know if you could reply you would tell me that I shouldn't be feeling that way, but if only I held you a few seconds in the bedroom and just let you leave for work, then maybe, just maybe, you wouldn't be in here."

The anticipated tears began to flow as expected as she shut her eyes tight and once again heard the familiar man's voice say, "Stay strong!" Nicole ignored it at first thinking it was her own thoughts of wanting Demetri to speak, until that moment it whispered, "I'm here with you."

Nicole looked up fast, every which way she could, trying to figure out where the voice came from, but had no idea since it seemed to come from every corner of the room. Thoughts began racing through her mind with all the possibilities of who or what the voice could be, but she only believed the one that made sense to her and that was her mind playing tricks on her. After looking around, Nicole looked back at Demetri and kissed him on his forehead.

"I love you!" Nicole said as she left the room, and then headed down to the main lobby where she came across Big Momma again. "Hey Mae Nell."

Big Momma looked over and saw Nicole walking toward her and said, "Hey honey, how have things been lately?"

"It's been hard, but I'm still making it."

"Just make sure you keep making it."

"So who is this handsome young man?"

"Oh, this is my youngest grandson Michael." When she introduced me I ducked behind her leg, after I started blushing.

"Aw, look at those dimples." Nicole said causing me to blush even more.

Big Momma laughed with her eyes halfway closed, causing her entire body to vibrate. "Michael, stop acting all shy. Come around here and stop hiding."

"I'm not hiding, Grandma," I said while smiling.

"Oh yeah, then what are you doing then?"

I looked at Nicole and then back up at Big Momma with what many would call a mischievous smile and said, "Um . . ."

The two of them enjoyed a nice laugh at my innocence and then Big Momma asked, "So what's been going on with you?"

"Well, I found out I was pregnant almost three weeks ago and when I came to share it with my husband I hoped he would finally awake, but he laid there. When I went home that night I thought, what if he never wakes up? Our son or daughter could grow up fatherless and that's the last thing I want for them."

"Child, you don't do that to yourself and lose your faith. You have to stay strong until your faith can stand trial."

"What do you mean?"

"Best way I can describe it is like the story of Abraham, when God told him to take his son and offer him as a sacrifice on Mount

Moriah. Abraham's faith was surely tested that day. After he obeyed, the angel of the Lord told Abraham not to touch his son because the Lord would provide his own sacrifice. So do you know that story?"

"Yes, ma'am, I do."

"Then you know that Abraham renamed the mountain Jehovah Jireh, meaning the Lord will provide."

Nicole smiled and said, "Yes, ma'am, I know that as well."

"Then just trust that God will provide and please child, do not call me ma'am, you're making me feel old."

"OK." Nicole said as she smiled, and her eyes began to glare from the collection of tears in her eyes. "Thank you Mae Nell, you just don't know how much your words have helped me." Nicole wrapped her arms around Big Momma tightly, closing her eyes feeling the warmth of her love.

Big Momma hugged Nicole back and said, "Honey, I'm just glad I can help. All the things I have told you I had to go through life to learn. That's why it's important to listen to the people who have been through them so you won't have to learn the hard way." When the two of them let go of each other I began to smile from the words that were said. "Well, Nicole, I have to get to this appointment so I'll be seeing you around OK?"

"Yes, ma'am!" Nicole said, and Big Momma gave her a funny look for calling her ma'am again, and then Nicole said, "I mean Mrs. Harris."

Big Momma and I finally arrived at her appointment for a routine checkup, and she was greeted by Dr. Trust. "Good morning Mae Nell, how are you doing today?"

Big Momma was all smiles since the Lord awakened her for another day. "I'm blessed as always Anthony, just taking one day at a time and doing whatever it is I can to help as many people as possible."

"Mrs. Harris, I thought we talked about you doing too much. You should be getting more rest."

"Anthony, I know we did talk about it, but that doesn't mean I'm going to stop. And like I mentioned in our last conversation, maybe you should start doing everything you can to help others."

Dr. Trust grinned and said sarcastically, "Mae Nell, you do know I'm a doctor right? Every day of my job is about doing everything I can to help. I'm just saying, I think it's in your best interest if you relax a little more."

"Oh yeah, and why is that? I'm not that sick where I have to sit still and do nothing."

"No, you aren't, but the way diabetes is, you might wake up one day and you won't be feeling that well. That's why it's best that you get as much rest as you can so you don't tire yourself out."

Big Momma immediately responded, not even allowing a breath in between the conversation. "Isaiah 53:5." She said and paused for a split second. "But He was wounded for our transgressions, he was bruised for our iniquities: the chastisement of our peace was upon Him; and with his stripes we are healed. Anthony, how long have I known you?" Big Momma asked.

"Since I was a kid, why?"

"Then you should know that I will not lie down to this disease. God has and always will take care of me and you should know that for yourself. Your mom and dad lived for God and loved Him with all of their hearts. You saw that every day of your life and—"

"And we both remember how that turned. The good Lord took them away." Dr. Trust said sarcastically, cutting her off because he was bothered from Big Momma talking about his parents. "Give me three good reasons why I should trust a God who took the three most important people in my life!" After his explosion he pulled himself together so things wouldn't get out of hand.

"I'll give you four: your mom, your dad, your brother and yourself." Dr. Trust looked at Big Momma but didn't reply. "Anthony, you know that God means the best for you, even if you have to hurt for a while. You and I both know that he will never give you more than you can handle."

"Well, we're all done here." Dr. Trust said.

Big Momma agreed and grabbed my hand. "You can't run from the Lord forever, Anthony. When He has a plan for your life He will continue to draw you near, one way or another. If you can't see it now then you will, just give it some time." She calmly said as the two of us exited the room.

When we went out the room, Dr. Trust looked up to the ceiling thinking, *Lord why did you have to place these people in my life?* During that train of thought he received a phone call. When he looked at the caller ID, to his surprise it was his pastor from his old church back home in Henderson, Nevada. *After all these years*, he wondered why he was receiving a call from him. *Maybe he's in town and wants to visit*, he thought, until he answered the phone.

"Hello." He answered, but by the time he pressed send on his cell phone to answer the call, it had already stopped ringing. Seconds later there was a message notification appearing on his phone.

He listened to the message and it said, "Hey Anthony, you already know who this is . . ." Dr. Trust knew exactly who it was, Joshua the pastor's son. "Yeah, this is Josh. I'm going to be in town helping a few churches the rest of this month all the way up until Thanksgiving, and I wanted to see if I could stay at your house so I won't have to spend the extra cash on a hotel. I know its short notice, but I figured you wouldn't mind since you did tell me if I'm ever in town I could stay with you." Joshua said sarcastically, "Well, I called and I have some things to tell you that have been happening in my life, and I was hoping we could talk like when you would help me out before. Anyway, give me a call back as soon as you can."

Dr. Trust had immediately called back and the two of them met at a restaurant a mile down the road from the hospital. The restaurant was an old-school diner only about one thousand square feet, painted in desert colors: sandy brown, cactus green, and sky blue. Inside was a bar-style counter with stools about four feet high and the seats around the diner were look-alikes of the backseat of a 1956 Plymouth Belvedere.

Dr. Trust arrived at the restaurant first and ordered them both a glass of water. He began looking around and saw a woman who he had performed heart surgery on nine years ago. As he recalled the surgery, thinking about the miracle that day, he saw Joshua pulling up in front of the restaurant and noticed a dent on the side his car. When Joshua entered the diner, the two of them immediately locked eyes and laughed after the many years of not seeing each other. Dr. Trust was about ten years older than Joshua, who was 27, and Joshua looked up to him when he first met him at church.

"Hey Josh, how have you been?" Dr. Trust greeted him with open arms like he was a little brother.

"I've been great, just taking one day at a time trying to survive."

"Yeah, I know what you mean. Every day for me has been hell it seems" Dr. Trust said.

"It can't be that bad."

"Man, you don't even know the half of it."

"Well then, start telling me the half I don't know."

"Always straight to the point with you." Dr. Trust stated, building the conversation as the two of them sat down in a booth looking at their menus. "OK, so you know I'm a doctor at the local hospital right?"

"Yeah, I don't see how you could do it. I know I couldn't." Joshua said.

"It can't be any harder than being a youth pastor having to deal with your dad as the senior pastor." As soon as he mentioned Joshua's dad, Dr. Trust noticed a sudden change in his posture. "Is everything all right?" he asked.

"Yeah, yeah. Everything is fine." Joshua nodded and said nervously with a slight smile on his face.

"You know if something's wrong you can always talk with me right? I mean you always did since you were five."

"Yeah, I will." Joshua whispered.

"All right then, so like I was saying, everybody who I've been talking to has been so in love with Jesus, and I'm not talking about going to church in love, I'm talking about in the word *in love*. These

three new patients of mine including everyone involved with—"
Dr. Trust stopped briefly as a female waitress came to take their
order, and he finally comprehended Joshua's response. "Wait, I will?"
Anthony interrupted himself, telling the waitress they needed a few
more minutes. "Sorry, I've been so caught up in my own little world
that I didn't hear what you said. So what's been happening?"

"No, that's OK." Joshua said with a slight chuckle. "But for starters
my dad passed away four nights ago around 3:00 a.m., he left the
church to me and I almost ran over a little boy two days ago, just a
few blocks away from that hospital you work at."

Dr. Trust suddenly realized that his problems weren't problems
at all, even though he was still unsatisfied with his current situation.

"Oh wow!" he answered. "How did your dad pass away?"

Joshua gathered himself after recalling the thought of his dad
being gone and just jumped straight to the end, not wanting to really
talk about it. "He died because it was his time."

"Old age, what do you mean?" Dr. Trust asked, knowing there
was more to what happened and became very curious of the cause.

"What else is there to say? His body failed after all these years of
being alive."

Dr. Trust could tell that he didn't want to talk about his dad
anymore, so he switched the subject, knowing he would talk when he
was ready, "So what happened with the kid you almost ran over?"

Joshua thought of what happened and replied. "God spoke to
me."

Dr. Trust didn't understand once more and asked, "What do you
mean God spoke to you? I know you can't seriously think that God
stopped you from almost killing that boy."

He sarcastically responded, "No, I know you aren't sitting here
in front of me, looking into my eyes, and telling me you believe God
didn't stop me. You were the main one who loved and lived for God
with all of your heart. I thought you would have been the one taking
over for my dad, but here you are, a big time, big paid doctor helping
sick people who prefer you over anybody else."

"Yeah, well, it's not what God had planned for me, but I definitely fell into this occupation."

Joshua became serious real fast after hearing Dr. Trust's remarks about God. "Are you sure this isn't what God had planned for you all along? Or you did know, but you don't want to admit that God chose the best for you, even though you've strayed so far away from Him?"

Dr. Trust grinned, jerking his head slightly up and exhaling through his nostrils. "Well, whether me or Him, I'd say I'm on the right path."

"Anthony." Joshua called to grasp his attention, "Do you still believe in God?"

Dr. Trust became silent for a brief moment so he could think. "Man, I'm not sure what to believe. It's like I know God is out there, but then at the same time so many horrible things have happened in my life and now . . . now I've seen so many horrific anonymities in my profession that argue against God being good at all, if He does exist. So if God is up there, why would I want to believe and trust someone who's letting all these terrible things happen in the world?"

Joshua thought out loud, "Now I know why that happened."

"Wait, why what happened?" Dr. Trust asked after not hearing him clearly.

Joshua exclaimed, "Me hitting that boy, or almost hitting him. I mean when I saw him literally right against my car and looked over to see his younger brother getting off the ground a few feet away, I thought it was only a miracle that the two of them were saved. But God spoke to me loud and clear after hearing you speak."

Dr. Trust looked at Joshua with the most confused look a person could have on their face and a smile just for fun.

"Don't look at me like I'm crazy." Joshua smiled knowing how he might sound.

"I'm still trying to grasp how you hitting or not hitting a boy, has anything to do with me."

"The older boy must have pushed the other one out of the way to save his life while only putting his self in harm's way. That would explain why he was picking himself up off the ground."

"OK, Sherlock Holmes, I see you putting puzzles together but that still doesn't explain anything."

"If you would stop interrupting then you would find out. God showed me something and I'm going to take heed to it. I know I'm supposed to help you but I don't see how that's possible." Joshua said jokingly.

Dr. Trust laughed quietly as the waitress returned, "Yeah, you don't make any sense." He joked, "We can talk about this later because I'm hungry. I haven't eaten in a day."

"I'll hold you to that, and we'll both see what I'm talking about sooner or later." Joshua said and then prayed to God, *Lord I need you to give me the wisdom and understanding of your will, and what I must do and say to Anthony so that I don't push him away. And Lord I ask that you bathe me with faith no matter how impossible this mountain may seem unmovable, in Jesus's name I pray, Amen!* The two of them ordered their food and began to reminisce about the last time they saw each other.

Chapter Nine

What You Thought Not, Is

Luke 18:27 (KJV)

"Jesus replied, "What is impossible with men is possible with God."

November 3, 2004

J oseph was sitting in a chair twirling his thumbs while patiently waiting for Dr. Trust to return with the x-rays that were taken of his head over his course of time being at the hospital. He then folded his hands, interlocking his fingers, and began to converse with God.

"OK Lord, I've been in this hospital almost an entire month now, because of a newly found tumor connected to my brain." Joseph inhaled deeply, "And you know, I was wondering what is going on. I mean I have never felt any signs of a tumor, no headaches, no depression or hearing loss and you know to be honest, if it wasn't for that I don't know how my faith would be in this situation. But you know I trust you anyhow."

At the time Joseph was talking to God, Dr. Trust was in the x-ray room looking at the pictures taken of Joseph's brain.

"Huh?" Dr. Trust said, placing the x-rays against the white board to see if what he was seeing was a mistake. He couldn't believe his eyes as his words began to scramble when spoke. "This can't be . . . I mean how, or what is this . . . There's just no way . . . I've never seen anything like this." Anthony stopped talking and thought, *Could it be?*

Dr. Trust finally arrived in Joseph's room with x-rays in hand, after much deliberation. "All right, Mr. Johnson," he said but was really unsure of how to tell Joseph what he saw in the x-rays.

"So what are the results?" Joseph asked after waiting in anticipation for Dr. Trust to return.

Dr. Trust walked over and clipped the X-Rays on the white board in order, from the time Joseph arrived to the most recent. "Are those all mine?" Joseph asked.

"Yes, these are all yours."

Joseph examined the tumor on his brain and asked, "So what's the verdict, Doc?"

Dr. Trust leaned his head slightly to the left. "Well, Joseph, these x-rays just don't look good at all." Dr. Trust paused to gather his thoughts of what to say next. "As you can see here on this first x-ray the tumor is clearly at its maximum size. But as you can see the tumor has gradually decreased in time."

"So what's happening exactly, am I tumor free?"

"Well, as much as I would love to say yes, you aren't exactly in the clear yet. Just because the tumor is decreasing in size does not mean that it's gone. But we will have to see what happens in the next couple weeks to determine anything that's abnormal."

"You know, Doc, I've been wondering, why exactly did you decide to keep me here at the hospital? I know I passed out and you found a tumor, but people live everyday with tumors. Why am I so different?"

Dr. Trust gave Joseph a silent stare only for a few seconds though before speaking. "When you were admitted into the hospital, I asked your wife Sarah if there was any condition you had that we needed to know about, and she told us no. We took you to x-ray the moment you arrived, and this is the first picture." Anthony brought out the first x-ray they took of Joseph.

"There's nothing there," Joseph said.

"Yes, I know, but this one here is just five hours later."

Dr. Trust pointed to the first x-ray he clipped up and the tumor was there. "Is that even possible? I mean are you sure that's five hours later and you didn't mix it up with another photo?"

"I'm positive Joseph. I couldn't even make sense of this myself, and now that the tumor is decreasing in size on its own, I really can't believe what I'm seeing." Dr. Trust then thought to himself, *How can you go from not having to having and then it gets three times smaller in less than a month?*

"So you're saying you've never heard of anything like this?"

"No, all the years in my profession and I have never seen anything like this, not even in a movie."

"Doc you said you believe in God right?"

"Yeah, but I don't see—"

"And didn't you say you didn't trust in God?" Joseph interrupted.

"Yeah, but that's besides the—"

"Then maybe you should start to believe again. It's like I said before, 'I cannot see, but I trust,'" Joseph said, interrupting again.

Dr. Trust smiled and shook his head, ignoring Joseph's last words. "All right Mr. Johnson today is your lucky day. I have contacted your wife and notified her that you are able to leave the hospital today. Now you do have to come in at least once a week for a checkup, just so we can see how you're coming along with your sickness."

"Sounds good." Joseph said, feeling sorry that he didn't get to have a real conversation with him.

Two hours later, Sarah arrived at the hospital and went straight to Joseph's room. She walked up behind Joseph, who was kneeling down at the side of the bed, praying.

"In Jesus's name I pray, Amen!" Joseph said, finishing his prayer.

"Hey baby." Sarah said full heartedly.

Joseph quickly turned after hearing Sarah's voice.

"Hey," he said with a smile, looking solely at her as he walked toward her. "I'm so happy to be finally coming home."

The two of them hugged each other immensely, touching their foreheads tightly together.

"I've missed you being home!" Sarah announced breathlessly. "I hope you have things all packed up so we can get out of here right away."

Joseph smiled as they pulled away from one another but still holding hands. He turned sideways and looked at the bed and then back to Sarah with a big grin on his face. "Well, let's go!" he exclaimed.

Sarah and Joseph exited the room and Joseph was relieved. When they walked down the hall Sarah noticed Big Momma leaving after visiting Demetri and praying with Nicole.

"Excuse me, Miss" Sarah said. Big Momma turned around after hearing Sarah's voice and Sarah said, "Do you remember me from a couple of weeks ago?"

Big Momma focused in on her face until it was clear to see. "Sarah is that you?" she said with a heart-filled smile. "Oh, it is you child. I was wondering when I was going to run into you again. I thought for sure your husband had gone home already."

Joseph grinned and said, "If only."

"And you must be Sarah's husband."

"Yes, ma'am, I am. I'm Joseph Johnson, and you are?"

"I'm Mae Nell Harris, and look how handsome you are." Sarah chuckled listening to Mae Nell boast about Joseph. "And you're so sweet, a real gentleman. I see why you're with this one." Big Momma said while looking at Sarah, causing Joseph to blush a little.

"Where are you headed?" Sarah asked Big Momma.

"I'm on my way to the main lobby to wait for my daughter Renee to give me a lift to the house."

"We could give you a ride if you don't mind." Joseph insisted.

"Oh, that's quite all right, but thank you anyway. My daughter is on her way with the boys and I haven't seen her oldest, Shawn, in I don't know how long. Every time they make a trip out this way, he is always doing something for his school, work, or playing in some sport."

"How old is that one?" Sarah asked while the three of them started walking to the elevator heading to the main lobby.

"He's eighteen, but you would never know it if you weren't told."

"Is he mature for his age?" Joseph asked.

"Actually, yes, he is very mature. He also doesn't look as young. I'm looking forward to seeing him again."

"I take it you're close to your family?" Joseph asked.

"There was a time when we were all very close. My daughter Renee and her oldest son, Shawn, aren't so talkative with me, but I am thankful for Isaiah and Michael. Those two boys keep my spirit high."

"They must be quite a handful."

Big Momma chuckled, "Yeah, they are. Always running around, always laughing, having a good time. I just pray that they do right by their mother and stay out of trouble."

Now exiting the elevator and entering the waiting area in the main lobby, Sarah said to Big Momma, "Mae Nell, so what's your impression on Dr. Trust?" Mae Nell looked at Sarah curiously, "I'm just asking because to me he seems like a good guy, but then there are times when he seems so lost in life. Like he's in a box and doesn't know how to get out. I'm worried about him."

"Child, don't you worry about Anthony. Yes, he is lost in his own mind right now, but there was a time when he knew God and had the utmost trust in Him. I know he still believes, but he is so busy trying to push God away that he is blind to see the beauty that God has been trying to unfold in his life."

Joseph gathered that Big Momma knew Dr. Trust for some time so he asked, "How long have you known him?"

"Oh, I've known that boy since he was in diapers." Big Momma chuckled. "His family moved from here to Nevada when he was twelve and he was so upset because his mother and father never discussed the move with him."

"I can imagine why he would be." Joseph stated and then continued, "I know if I was him I would have at least wanted my parents to give me some kind of notice. He had to have been devastated not being able to say goodbye to any of his friends."

"Oh, he was." Big Momma confirmed, "But it wasn't so much the move that took it out of him."

"What do you mean?" Sarah asked.

"About two weeks before they moved away, Anthony's younger brother, CJ, had bled to death in this very hospital after being shot. His lung was punctured and the doctor couldn't reach the bullet in enough time to save him. How different things would have been if that doctor would have been able to save that boys life, we will never know."

"Is that why he became a doctor, to save people?" Sarah asked.

"Yes, honey, I believe it is. Though he has been blessed as a doctor, it saddens me because he sees all these people daily and helps them, but he has not yet been able to come to peace after all these years from the death of his brother."

Joseph wanted to know more about Dr. Trust's past, but he decided not to ask. Instead, his mind wandered offtrack thinking where Big Momma's ride was, "Where's your daughter at?"

Big Momma looked at her watch and started to wonder the same. "I'm sure she'll be here soon."

"Would you like us to wait here with you? We really don't mind at all." Sarah stated.

"No, that's quite all right. I don't want to burden the two of you with the lateness of my daughter. And besides, the two of you have a lot of catching up to do."

They smiled at one another and then Joseph said, "Mae Nell, we really don't mind. Neither one of us has a thing to do today. And besides, we have the rest of our lives to spend together. Spending a little time with someone who took their own time to help my wife will not be a burden."

Big Momma smiled joyfully. "Well, I appreciate the two of you staying with me. I don't have many people around who care this much beside my daughter and her—" She paused and looked up to the door, where she saw her oldest grandson, Shawn, enter with hopelessness on his face. He walked over to the front desk where he asked the nurse if she had seen his grandmother Mae Nell. Joseph and Sarah noticed the heartache growing in Big Momma's face as Shawn nodded his head, telling the nurse thank you, after she pointed him in the direction of Big Momma.

"Is everything all right?" Joseph asked.

"Yeah, everything is going to be just fine." Big Momma stated. "You two can go ahead and leave if you'd like. It looks like my ride is here."

Sarah kindly spoke, "Mae Nell, we're going to stay here and make sure everything is all right with your grandson."

Big Momma thanked Sarah and Joseph for their willingness to stay with her and stood to her feet as Shawn arrived in front of her.

"Hi." Shawn greeted Joseph and Sarah with a sense of urgency, not taking time to introduce himself properly. "Grandma, are you ready?" he asked, reaching for her arm to walk her to the car.

Big Momma gently pulled her arm away and asked, "Shawn, why are you looking like that, and where is your mother?"

"She sent me to pick you up."

"OK, so where is she at?"

Shawn was unsure what to say so he insisted that she hurried. "Grandma, come on! We haven't got all day."

Joseph and Sarah watched on as Shawn continued to push Big Momma to leave.

"Shawn stop it and tell me the truth right now." At that moment, Shawn's eyes began to tear up, but he didn't say a word. "Shawn, tell Big Momma what happened." He looked her sincerely in the eyes as she continued, "Please!"

"She's gone!" Shawn whispered.

Big Momma wasn't quite sure what he meant so she asked again. "What do you mean exactly?"

"She's gone!" Shawn yelled, drawing the attention of the few people in the waiting room. "She's gone and I don't know when she's coming back," he said, leaning into Big Momma's arms. "And I don't understand why."

Big Momma became frantic and her heart sped up a little as she held Shawn tightly. "Honey, I need you to be strong OK? Please explain to me exactly how she is gone."

Shawn slowed his breathing as best he could and tried to explain. "All I saw ... She ... I just don't know exactly. One minute, my mom was walking to me after I exited the plane, and the next, she was gone."

At that moment, Big Momma was a little confused, not sure what he was talking about. Sarah walked closer behind Big Momma and planted her hand gently on her shoulder. "Is everything OK?" Sarah asked.

Big Momma nodded her head and asked Shawn. "Where is your brother Isaiah?"

Almost unable to speak, Shawn squeezed the words out. "He's in the car."

"Sarah, would you mind driving us home? And Joseph, would you be able to follow us in your car?"

"Yes, ma'am, we can do that." Joseph answered. "Anything you need just ask, and we will do our best to do so."

"Thank you Joseph, that means a lot to me that you would do this." She said thinking about where Renee could've gone. Sarah wrapped one arm around Big Momma's shoulders and walked her to the car. Once they entered the car, Big Momma looked at Sarah and her eyes were filling with tears. Without the tears, Sarah was unable to tell how sad Big Momma was.

"Everything is going to be fine." Sarah repeated Big Momma's words from earlier. "If you need me to look after the boys for a few days, I can. It's no problem really!"

Big Momma pulled a handkerchief out of her pocket and spotted the tears coming from her eyes. "Thank you, Sarah. I wish I had the words to tell you how much I'm grateful for you and Joseph and all the help in such an abrupt fashion."

"It's no problem at all, and like I said earlier, if there is anything that you need one of us to do please don't hesitate to ask!"

Big Momma grabbed ahold of Sarah's hand, closed her eyes and softly said, "In Jesus's name!" She then placed her hands atop her lap and said, "God give me the strength."

Chapter Ten

Love and Forgiveness

Ephesians 4:31-32 (KJV)

Let all bitterness, and wrath, and anger, and clamor, and evil speaking, be put away from you, with all malice: And be ye kind one to another, tenderhearted, forgiving one another, even as God for Christ's sake hath forgiven you.

"Robert, I'm sorry. I can't do this anymore." Elise said, hoping his feelings weren't hurt.

Robert heard the sound of his heart crushing as he dropped a dark blue box he was holding in his right hand. His thoughts flashed back to all the beautiful moments the two of them shared.

"Robert, say something!" Elise demanded as she noticed the box hitting the ground. Robert's eyes dropped, his posture stiffened as he turned his back to her. "Please, talk to me. Turn around, baby!"

"Baby?" Robert questioned after quickly turning around. "How could you call me baby? The sound of hearing that after what you just said hurts."

"It's a habit I guess."

"Are you serious, a habit?"

Elise didn't want to say anything else because she knew Robert's heart was already torn apart because hers was as well.

"Why are you doing this to us?" Robert asked.

Elise shook her head while tears flowed down her face. "We weren't even together Robert."

"How were we not together? We spent every waking moment together and you're telling me we weren't together."

"I'm sorry Robert."

"So what about last week when we talked. You mean that wasn't real."

"It was but . . . we just can't be together."

Elise took off the necklace Robert's father gave to him and held her hand out to give it back. When Robert reached out his hand and took the necklace, he closed his eyes and tears began to build up.

"At least tell me why?"

"I'm . . ." Elise stopped. She wanted to tell Robert why, but she knew it was best if she didn't. "I can't."

"You know what ..." Robert didn't finish talking because he didn't want to say the wrong thing so he turned and walked away, clutching the necklace tightly in his fist. Elise just stood there, she then looked to the ground and saw the blue box Robert dropped, sitting at her feet. She picked it up and looked inside. *It's the most beautiful ring I've seen*, Elise thought and she couldn't believe she hurt him like that.

Lord I don't know what I just did, but I ask that you make things OK. Help Robert find it in his heart to forgive me because I know it won't be easy. Lord I know one day he will find out why I did this, but until that day comes I ask that you help him see that I did this for the two of us. I didn't want to ruin his life. God I pray this in Jesus's name, Amen!

November 5, 2004

Robert and Malcolm were sitting down watching cartoons on TV. "All right Mac, it looks like it's about time for bed." Robert said.

"Ah, man, already?" Malcolm whined, leaning his body against Robert's arm.

"Yeah, man." Robert said and laughed.

"Can I finish this show, pleeease!"

Robert smiled while shaking his head, saying, "I don't know. You need to get some rest because I'm taking you to your grandma's house bright and early so she can take you to church."

"How come I can't just go with you?"

"I think it's best if you go with your grandma."

"Why?"

"Well, because I don't know any churches to go to."

"But we can look for one together." Malcolm began to think of churches he's seen nearby. "Oh, what about the big church on the hill in Barstow, that's where my mom used to take me when we would come visit grandma."

"I ... I don't know." Robert hesitated to say. "I just think it's best for you to go with your grandma. You're closer to her."

"But I want to go with you!" Malcolm whined. "I like being around you."

Robert thought for a second if he should take Malcolm to church since he hadn't been in one for years, but after thinking about it he decided not. "You can finish this show, but after that I want you to go to bed so you won't be tired."

"We'll finish this conversation when my show is over." Malcolm insisted before falling sound asleep just ten minutes later, at 9:28, only a couple of minutes before his show ended.

Robert stood to his feet after he heard Malcolm's light snore. He guided his hands and arms underneath him, lifting him up off the couch and carrying him to the room. After tucking him in the bed, Robert kneeled and watched Malcolm sleeping peacefully.

"Ever since you've been here, I've been feeling brand new. I don't know why but I have."

While looking at Malcolm, Robert's mind was overwhelmed with the familiarity of his face. *He reminds me of someone,* Robert thought to himself, only to come to no explanation of who the boy looked like.

Robert hung his head low, with his eyes closed and whispered without thinking, "Thank you God." He immediately lifted off the ground, standing upright, and then looking around the room. As he shook his head, the doorbell rang. Robert walked to the door wondering who it could be, and when he arrived and opened it there was no one there. He looked out the door to the left and right, but there was no one or anything to see except for a stray cat walking down the street.

Robert then closed the door, locked it, and walked back to the couch to lie down and watch more cartoons. Half an hour later, Robert's phone rang in his pocket. He was startled from the sound of the ringer after having the volume set to its max.

"Hello." He answered after pulling the phone out of his pocket.

"Hi, I'm trying to reach Robert Brown." A man on the other end said.

"Yeah, this is him." Robert said as he sat up and placed one of his elbows on a knee to prop his head up with his hand.

"I'm Officer Hernandez." The man introduced.

"What can I do for you?"

"Well, your phone number was the last incoming call in her phone."

"Who's phone?" Robert questioned.

"Elise Aniela Magnano's phone."

Robert's heart then stopped at the sound of her name. A blank stare covered his face as he worried. "Where is she at?"

"Um . . ." Officer Hernandez started, not sure of how to tell him. "Well, that's what I called for. We found Ms. Magnano in an alley covered with blood and cuts on her body. We are not sure how she was killed, but at first glance all signs point to her being a rape victim. Once we receive the autopsy reports, we will be able to investigate the situation further."

"Wait." Robert paused trying to gather the information received. "This isn't happening."

"Mr. Brown, I'm sorry that your girlfriend has been . . ."

"She wasn't my girlfriend." Robert said in the nicest possible way, trying not to sound like he didn't care because he really did.

"I'm sorry, I truly am. But I was just calling you to give you report of your friend's death. We thought it would be important if you knew." Officer Hernandez politely responded. "I know this isn't easy to hear, but just know that we are going to do everything we can to find out what happened to her. I give you my word."

"Thank you Officer."

"Oh, but there is one thing that we found on her possession that I believe she wanted you to know."

"Yeah, and what's that?"

"It's a letter about her son."

As soon as Robert heard about the letter, he sprung out of his sleep and his shirt was covered with sweat. He looked around until he came to reality after figuring out it was just a dream. He sat up on the couch thinking about Elise and where in the world she could be.

"Oh God!" Robert paused. "I need to know where Elise is. You're the only one I know who is in contact with her. I pray you bring her home in Jesus's name, Amen!"

After praying, he got off the couch and went to his room where Malcolm was sound asleep. Robert kneeled to the side of the bed, planted his elbows and folded his hands to pray. *It's been a long time since I've done this,* he thought to himself. He closed his eyes and began, "Lord, the last time we spoke I know it wasn't on good terms. I was so upset at you for allowing everything special to me to be taken out of my life. And Lord even today . . ." He stopped to gather his composure. "Today I . . . I still feel as if you left me. I've been alone for all these years after the death of my parents, and then, the neglect of me from the one person left on this earth I still loved. I miss You, Lord. Every single moment of everyday has been hell for me. All those years ago, I would have never thought for a second that I would have lived, not even one day, without bringing You with me. But here I am, eight long years without so much as a hello. I feel so confused about what happened all those years ago and even though I left without You, I have always known deep down in my heart that You had never left me, not even one second." The tears that built up in his eyes started to pour out after the emotions that he's been holding in had finally released in an instance. "Lord, I don't want to be alone anymore. I'm tired of fighting You and everyone who tries to become a part of my life. Lord even Demetri, through him I have seen Your one-of-a-kind love and it tore me up inside every day because I wanted You back. All this time I knew where I was supposed to be and it took meeting Demetri Thomas and now little Malcolm to guide me here to my knees." Robert wiped the tears away from his face as he clenched his eyes and fist tighter, no longer gripping his hands together. "Lord I know you already know, but the main reason I'm here is because of the dream I just had. It was scary, and hearing that Elise died hurt me because the last thing I want is for Malcolm to be alone."

As Robert continued to pray, a little hand grabbed ahold of his, "I won't be alone because I have you!" Malcolm said after waking up to Robert's praying.

Robert lifted his head after hearing Malcolm's voice and gripped his hands as tight as he could. "Did God and I wake you up?"

Malcolm nodded, "Yes, you two did."

"We're sorry. I don't even know why I came in here to pray."

"It's OK. I'm used to hearing my mommy praying at night too."

"Did she pray a lot?"

"Yeah, mostly about you. I would always hear her say your name and would wonder who she was talking about. But now I know." Malcolm said innocently.

"Really?"

"Yeah, she always asked God to help you forgive her. I don't know why, I guess she did something bad to you." Robert wasn't able to think of anything to say before Malcolm became curious and asked, "Can you tell me a story about you and my mom when you two were friends?"

"Um, I really don't know."

"Pretty please, with sugar on top."

"Why do you want to know anyways?" Robert asked with a smile.

"I just want to know what my mommy was like when she was younger is all."

"You need to be sleep." Robert chuckled. "But your mom, she was a sweet person."

"Then how come she wants you to forgive her?"

Robert then smiled, seeing where this conversation would lead to. "You ask a lot of questions little guy."

"How else can I expand my mind?" Malcolm asked while lying on his side, propping his head up with his hand.

Robert, still kneeling down with his elbows on the bed, began to laugh, "You are too much."

"So are you going to tell me about her?"

Robert stood to his feet and said, "Scoot over."

Malcolm slid from the middle of the bed to the farthest side away from Robert, and Robert sat halfway on the bed, leaning against the headboard with one leg hanging off to the side.

"Your mom has and forever will be one of the sweetest people I've ever known."

"How long have you known her?"

"Since I was a little older than you." Robert informed. "I met your auntie Ashley first, when she helped me and my bike off the ground. Then I met your mom shortly after. I'll never forget the moment when she called out to Ashley for her to come home to assist her with dyeing her hair."

"Is that why her hair is red?"

Robert chuckled. "No, actually her hair is naturally that red color. If I hadn't been there that day, her hair would've been black."

"Oh, I'm glad she didn't go through with it. She wouldn't be as pretty if her hair wasn't red."

Robert laughed aloud while shaking his head. "Yeah, that's kind of what I told her to make her change her mind about dyeing her hair."

"How close were you and my mom?"

"Your mother and I were the best of friends from the first day we met all the way through high school."

"You and my mommy were in love weren't you?"

Robert smiled, shocked to hear how smart this boy became as the time went by. "What made you ask that?"

"Because when you talk about my mom, you have the same look that she has when she tells me about you."

"So then you already know everything I'm telling you then?"

"Well, kind of. I'm only asking you to see what parts my mom left out when she told me this story, but so far it seems she told me everything."

"You don't trust your mom?"

"I trust her, but let's be real, she's a woman."

Robert smiled but giggled to himself. "Yeah, I know what you mean. Women can be trouble, but I thank God for them."

Malcolm became curious while Robert was speaking and kind of cut him off. "Are you still in love with my mommy?"

Robert took a deep breath with a little nervousness, shaking his head and wasn't sure how to answer. "Why do you ask?"

"I just want to know is all, eyes can't tell the story of the heart. A lot of times you have to look within a person to see what they're about."

"You must have learned that from your mom." Robert said as he scooted his entire body on the bed, still leaning his head against the headboard. "Your mom always did know how to see right through people." he stated.

"Yeah, she does."

"So what about your dad?" Robert asked. But Malcolm didn't know how to answer, he just turned his head to the right to look away from Robert.

"I don't know." he whispered.

"Have you ever seen him?"

"And you said I ask a lot of questions." Malcolm giggled trying to avoid the question.

Robert noticed as much, so he leaned slightly closer to him. "I'm just trying to get to know you more, is all."

"Yeah, I know." Malcolm said with a smile, looking up to Robert. "But no, I don't know who he is. My mom always told me how great of a guy he was and how he would love to see me. I don't know why she won't tell me who he is."

"What if I helped you find him."

"Well . . . I don't know if I want to him know now."

"Why wouldn't you want to know him? If your mom says he's a good guy then I'm sure he is."

"Yeah, but I might not like him. He might not be as cool as you are."

There was a few seconds pause in the conversation before Robert responded. "I'm sure your father is a lot cooler than I am. I'm not someone who most people like to be around."

"Is that because of my mom?"

Robert's face became still; no motion at all after his eyes closed. He slid down on to his back to place his head on the pillow. "Yeah. I mean not just her." Robert said, relieving his lungs from holding his breath without realizing it. "I know you might not understand, but then again you are pretty smart. I just kind of put a shell up around my heart and it holds me back from forgiveness."

"Why don't you remove it?"

"I've tried, but I've lost too many people who were close to me and because I don't ever want to take that chance of being hurt again, the shell kind of just stayed."

"Well, I think you should try again." Malcolm said, expressing his want to be closer to him. "My mom always says that people will surprise you if you let them, good or bad. And the only reason people leave your life is because they are like a leaf on a tree."

Robert smiled, hearing that analogy from Elise before. "Your mother did a great job with you."

"What do you mean?"

"Raising you on her own, she taught you very well. You're what only five? And you are definitely the smartest little boy I know."

"She'd be happy to hear that."

"Any parent would." Robert began thinking of Elise's whereabouts. "So did your mom happen to tell you where she went?"

"No, she just told me she was going to drop me off at her friend's house and that she'll be back."

"Don't take this the wrong way because I've actually enjoyed you being here a lot more than I thought I would, but did she happen to say when she was coming back?"

"No, I didn't bother to ask. I love my mom and I know she wouldn't put me in harm's way, that's why I wasn't scared when she left me with you." Malcolm's eyes finally closed as he snuggled closer against Robert and said, "Oh, and if you're getting closer to me, it's OK, because I'm not going to leave out of your life. I promise!"

A couple of tears began to fall from Robert's eyes slowly after he began to feel a love that he hadn't felt for so long. "Thank you." Robert said sincerely as he too closed his eyes until the two of them both fell sound asleep.

Chapter Eleven

Asleep but Awake

Isaiah 57:2 (KJV)

*He shall enter into peace: they shall rest in their
beds, each one walking in his uprightness.*

November 7, 2004

Nicole entered Demetri's hospital room, crying as tears soaked select spots on her shirt. She walked slowly, with her head slumped down, and fell to the floor next to the bed. She couldn't control her emotions at this point, and it caused her to curl her body together in the fetal position. She then closed her eyes tightly, thinking about what she just experienced, and it was so unbearable to her that she wasn't able to be comforted by the loving and caring arms of her husband. Dr. Trust was coming from tending to another patient next door when he saw Nicole lying on the floor, crying shamelessly. Dr. Trust walked over to Nicole and tapped her on the arm to get her attention.

"Nicole." he called, but there was no answer. "Let me help you." Nicole started to have trouble breathing, so she allowed him to help her up into a nearby chair next to where Demetri was lying in a coma. When she sat down, Dr. Trust asked, "What's going on?"

Nicole chose not to answer because she didn't want to talk with anyone except for Demetri. And because of that, she shied away from Dr. Trust saying, "Can you leave, please? I just need to talk to my husband." Nicole said as calmly as she could.

"Yeah," he said, confused, after just getting off the phone with her minutes before she arrived at the hospital. "I'll just come back and check on you in a few," he said, as he paced backward toward the door, then turned and walked away.

When Nicole could feel the presence of Dr. Trust leaving, she just watched Demetri lying in bed for a few minutes before speaking.

"I need you!" Nicole testified her loneliness, now looking at the floor instead of Demetri. "You don't know how hard this is for me. To be alone and need someone to at least be there." She stopped for a second to look at her phone that was vibrating in her purse. After seeing it was the officer who she spoke with prior to arriving at the hospital, she decided to call him back later. "Baby, I really need you!"

she exclaimed, walking to the side of the bed, only a foot away, and placed her hand gently on his forehead, running her fingers through his hair. "It's almost your favorite holiday, only about three weeks left. We were invited to someone's house for Thanksgiving dinner if you wake up before then. Her name is Mae Nell Harris. I know you don't know who she is yet, but she has been so wonderful to me, especially when I need someone to talk to." Nicole smiled, thinking about how nice Big Momma had been to her so far. "I can't wait until the day when the two of you meet. I'm sure you two will get along very well, just talking about God all day."

One of the nurses entered the room quietly and said, "Mrs. Thomas," Nicole looked over at the nurse. "Would you like to spend the night with your husband? It is getting pretty late."

Nicole looked at the time and saw it was closing in on midnight. All the soaking she did in the car must have really passed time.

"Yes, I would like that." she answered.

The nurse nodded and brought an extra blanket and pillow and then reclined the chair in the room. "Don't worry, Mrs. Thomas, this chair is one of the most comfortable ones in any of the rooms. You should rest well throughout the night."

"Thank you. I really appreciate all of this."

The nurse smiled, "You are very welcome." There's a short pause as the nurse took a breath. "Now if you need anything, you just walk over next to your husband and press the nurse button on that remote over there and I will be right over as soon as I can."

"Thank you!" Nicole smiled.

"You're welcome."

"Do you recommend eating the food here in the cafeteria?"

The nurse giggled. "The food in the cafeteria is very good. I don't know what's so different at this hospital, but the food will be satisfying no matter what you decide to eat."

"Thank you again." Nicole said.

"You have a wonderful night, and remember, the button."

Nicole giggled softly, grateful for the welcoming hospitality. "OK, I won't." The nurse left and Nicole kissed Demetri on the forehead and on the lips before sitting in the chair under the blanket. "Good night, baby! I love you!"

Two hours earlier, late in the night, Jennifer, Sarah's assistant manager at Generational Beauty, was closing up shop for Sarah so she could be at home with Joseph for the night. A Hispanic male wearing a black hoodie and dark-colored jeans entered the store exactly one minute before they would usually lock the doors at 10:00 p.m.

"Hello, sir!" Jennifer greeted the man. "I'm sorry but we're closing at this moment. We reopen doors again at eight tomorrow morning if you'd like to come back then."

The man lifted his head slightly, sweeping off his hood, appearing troubled. Jennifer was ending the transaction for her last customer of the day, Nicole, when the man looked toward the exit door behind him.

"Sir, are you OK?" Nicole asked after noticing the man continuing to look around as if he was unsure of where he was.

He nodded quickly and looked away, pulling his lips inward while he reached behind his back into his waistband. "I'm sorry, I don't want any trouble." He said in a soft, scared voice, focusing on Jennifer.

"Sorry for what?" Jennifer asked as she handed Nicole her bag of clothes and the $3.16 in change left over from the purchase.

The man brought his hand around slowly, holding a Smith & Wesson 9 mm handgun and walked up to Nicole first, pointing toward her chest.

"Get on the floor, please!" The man said nervously, trying to keep the gun from shaking. "I said get on the floor!" he yelled louder, as fear crept upon the two women.

"Jesus, help!" Nicole said as she slowly descended to the ground, still holding her change and the bag in opposite hands. Jennifer was frozen still from the fear of possibly being shot.

"Open the register." The man demanded, now pointing the gun at Jennifer and throwing an empty bag to her raised hands. "I need . . . give me all the money," he said with a stutter, constantly looking behind him. "Come on hurry up!" he started to become frustrated watching Jennifer dropping money while she placed it in the bag. The man moved around to the back of the counter with the gun pointed in the air and pushed Jennifer out of the way. "Move!" he said as she hit the ground.

The man forgot Nicole was on the other side of the counter as he loaded the money into the bag. She carefully reached into her purse and pulled out her phone to text Dr. Trust, hoping he would call the police and tell them Generational Beauty was being robbed and she was there. She didn't know who else to text except for him.

Dr. Trust received the text seconds later and called the police immediately. "Barstow PD, this is dispatch."

"Hi, my name is Dr. Anthony Trust of Barstow Hospital. I just received a text from a friend who said Generational Beauty is being robbed at this moment."

"What is your friend's name?"

"Nicole Thomas. Her husband is a patient here at the hospital."

"Did she give you any description of the person committing the robbery?"

Dr. Trust hesitated. "Um . . . I don't know. The one holding the gun I guess. All she told me was the place is being robbed."

"OK thank you Dr. Trust. We have units in the area that will check it out."

"Thank you!" He said, hanging up the phone.

Back at the store, the man was finishing loading the bag with money and demanded Jennifer to lie on the floor next to Nicole. Both of them were scared, but Jennifer was still in shock. She couldn't hold herself together as tears poured from her eyes.

"Get her under control. Please!" he added compassionately.

Nicole moved slowly toward Jennifer, reaching her arms out to her. "Everything is going to be fine."

Because of all the yelling and the shock that hit her body, Jennifer became very emotional and began to panic, waving her hand side to side in front of her mouth. "I can't breathe, I can't breathe!"

The man observed as Jennifer was leaning against Nicole's leg on her back. Nicole was holding the back of Jennifer's head, whispering in her ear. "Calm down," he said, looking around the store cautiously. Then in an instant, he dropped the bag of money and walked toward Jennifer and Nicole. Nicole was frightened, not sure what was about to happen until he spoke.

"Here let me." he offered.

Nicole couldn't believe what she was seeing. This was the same man who had pointed a gun at the two of them, screaming and then pushing Jennifer to the floor. Because of that, Nicole gave him a look of distrust and shook her head no. He looked in his hand and saw he was still holding the gun. So he tucked the gun in the back of his waistband once more and placed one hand on Jennifer's chest.

"Jesus!" The man cried, drawing Nicole's attention to him before repeating himself twice more.

Nicole's eyes widened after hearing God's name come from his mouth. She was once again in disbelief, wondering how he could do so much bad and then have the nerves to call on Jesus.

The man continued to repeat himself, "Jesus! Jesus! Jesus!" After each breath he took, he would say Jesus three times. Nicole was still looking strangely at the man until she heard Jennifer speak.

"Jesus!" Jennifer whispered with the man. Her breathing slowly began to return to normal with each call of the name Jesus. Minutes later, when Jennifer was able to breathe a little better, the man looked sincerely into Nicole's eyes, "I'm sorry, I had too."

The roaring sounds of police sirens seemed to hit on cue when he finished his apology. The man stood to his feet, walking toward the front entrance, passing the bag of money without hesitation. After nearing the store entrance, he lifted his hands and eyes toward heaven, dropping to his knees. "I'm sorry Lord . . . I'm sorry." he cried.

Nicole watched the man as he knelt to his knees, bent over, apologizing. Jennifer was still being held on the ground by Nicole as her breathing had inched its way back to normal. The police arrived, and from what they could see from outside, they assessed the situation inside the store and then proceeded forward toward the door with caution. One of the officers entered the store after seeing the man who robbed the store, kneeling on the floor. The officer pulled his sidearm out, not knowing if the man was still armed.

"Place your hands on the ground and lay flat on your stomach." The man didn't even look at the officer that spoke, but he did as he was asked without hassle. "Put your hands behind your back." The officer demanded. The man continued to cry as the officers searched him, finding the gun in the back of his waistband. The officer handed the weapon to another officer who was there to assist and placed handcuffs tightly around the man's wrist. "You have the right to remain silent. Anything you say can and will be used against you in a court of law. You have the right to an attorney. If you cannot afford an attorney, one will be appointed for you." The man nodded, understanding his Miranda rights, and was taken into custody by the second officer. Jennifer was now sitting upright on her own, talking with Nicole when the officer walked over to take a statement.

"Hi, I am Officer Ryan James. I need to get statements from the two of you. Can you tell me what happened?" Officer James asked, looking at Nicole first.

"What all did you need to know?" Nicole asked.

Officer James chuckled softly. "Well, I need to know everything the both of you saw. At least what you can remember, so if you don't mind starting from the beginning that would be great."

"Well, he came in with a gun and asked for all the money." Nicole stated.

"OK, I need you to give me specifics: If threatened you in any way, if he put his hands on you. I need any and everything this man did while he was here."

Jennifer immediately remembered how he calmed her down, while Nicole thought first of everything wrong he did.

"He entered the store quietly." Nicole said to start. "Then he yelled, wanting Jennifer to open the register and empty the money into the bag." Nicole goes further into detail, telling Officer James just about every grueling thing that had happened that night. Well, that is, everything except for how he gave himself up to the police so he could be human and help someone in need.

"What about what he did?" Jennifer asked Nicole curiously, not understanding why she wouldn't mention the end of the event.

Officer James turned his attention to Jennifer. "What exactly did he do?"

Nicole shook her head, not wanting Jennifer to say anything because she wanted the man to get everything she felt he deserved. "He helped me." Jennifer stated.

"What do you mean he helped you?"

Jennifer's nerves began to overflow her body. "She left out the part when he calmed me down when I was having a panic attack."

"Was he who caused the attack?" Officer James queried.

"Well, yes, but . . ." Jennifer took a pause after stumbling over her words. "What I'm trying to say is if it wasn't for him calming me down, I don't know what would have happened to me."

Officer James's eyebrows rose in curiosity, "So he helped you?" he inquired.

"Yes, he did."

"Is this true, ma'am?" he asked Nicole.

"Yes," she said shamelessly.

"All right, so . . ." Officer James started. "What was the reason he decided to help again?"

"I don't know. He was on his way out the door with the money, when he stopped and turned around."

"OK, well, I believe that is all. If there is anything else I need, I will give one of you a call."

Officer James finished getting all the information possible from the two ladies and left them alone. Jennifer beamed strongly at Nicole. "How come you did that?" she asked.

"Did what?" asked Nicole, already having an idea of what she was talking about.

"Why didn't you tell the officer the only nice thing that man did? It's like you tried to force the hand of the law."

"I did what I felt should've been done," Nicole said. "Did you forget he pointed a gun directly at the both of us? He deserves everything that is coming to him."

"I don't believe so."

"Oh, and why don't you believe that?"

"If you would've looked past the gun and the yelling, you would've been able to see within' that man's heart. He wasn't doing something he wanted to do."

Nicole couldn't believe what she was hearing, and wondered what other nonsense was going to come out of Jennifer's mouth.

"Every time he spoke . . ." Jennifer hesitated. "He didn't seem like he wanted to do it at all. I know what he did was wrong and I had that panic spell, but he was so compassionate when he came back and prayed with me."

"But he caused it." Nicole affirmed. "This entire mess was his fault, no matter what he did in the end."

"I know, I know, it was his fault. But the fact that he turned around to help was enough for me to believe he had a good heart, and it should be enough for you as well. While I didn't like what he did, I do forgive him. This store's manager, Sarah, always tells me to forgive no matter what the person did."

"And you're able to do that in this situation?"

"Yes, because the forgiveness isn't for the person you're forgiving, it's for you. It may take me awhile to completely forgive him, but it's something I need to do, so the weight from not forgiving isn't wearing me down."

"I applaud you on that." Nicole said sarcastically." "But still, I don't see how you can forgive him."

Jennifer looked directly into her eyes. "It's only possible if the love of God overtook your hurt, hate, and pain."

First Mae Nell and now this young girl, God, if you're trying to tell me, please let me know. Am I not doing something right? Nicole thought to herself and sighed. "I have to get out of here. I have to go see my husband," she said.

On her way out the door with her shopping bag in hand, the recent events took a big toll on her as she tried to forget it even happened. But how easy is it to forget about a gun being pointed at you, and go on about the rest of your night as if nothing happened?

Silence was all Jennifer could think of as she thought of things to say to Nicole after her abrupt decision to leave. Jennifer immediately called Sarah, hoping to reach her so there wouldn't be a surprise if Officer James called or arrived anytime soon. Sarah didn't answer the phone though, because she was asleep after being worn out from helping Big Momma with her two youngest grandchildren, me and Isaiah. Since there was no answer, Jennifer left a message, locked up the store, and headed home with nothing but thoughts of the night's events.

Chapter Twelve

You Can Handle It

Isaiah 41:10 (KJV)

Fear thou not; for I am with thee: be not dismayed; for I am thy God: I will strengthen thee; yea, I will help thee; yea, I will uphold thee with the right hand of my righteousness.

November 14, 2004

"I can't do this! There's no way I can." Dr. Trust asserted. "I mean, how can someone have such a burden to carry that is nothing less than punishment?"

Dr. Trust couldn't fathom these unseen, unheard-of events in the past couple of weeks. He felt that he was being unfairly punished by God and began to go on a rant, targeting his anger toward Joshua.

"I know what you're going through." Joshua offered his understanding.

"No, you don't. You don't have the slightest clue of how hard it is to want to help someone, but you can't because you have no idea how to."

Joshua turned all his attention totally toward him, not giving the slightest hint of abandonment. "Anthony, you're going to sit here and tell me that, with all that I have been through in this past month: my dad passing away, me almost running over some kid, and now I'm here, trying to help you see that you are capable of doing all things through Christ who strengthens you."

"There you go again." Dr. Trust complained.

"There I go again?" Joshua questioned. "I'm trying to help you. There are people all throughout this entire hospital that could use your help so you can't let this one patient be such a burden. Just because you don't understand all that is happening with him, that doesn't justify you giving up and quitting on them."

The awkward silence cut through the air as they gazed intently at one another. "Why did you become a doctor again?" Joshua asked. "Wasn't it to help those in need?" Dr. Trust sat there with an empty look in his face, like he was lost in space, seeing where this conversation was going. "After your brother died, you made this gift that God bestowed within your hands and transformed it into a burden which you hold today. I know that you never let go, you never forgave the man who shot him or God for that matter, and now after all these years of holding on to those feelings you are being digested by them." Dr. Trust was frozen by the truth as he continued to listen. "Anthony, you need to forgive that man, and forgive God so you can be free of the pain."

"How?" Dr. Trust shouted. "There's no possible way for me to forgive someone who is dead."

"He's dead? For how long?"

Dr. Trust looked to the ground, disturbed.

"You didn't kill him did you?"

"What? No, I didn't kill him. He was involved in the same car accident that my coma patient, Demetri Thomas, was in."

"You can still forgive him, but only when you choose. All you have to say is I forgive you, and mean it from the heart."

Dr. Trust moved his eyes around the room, trying to avoid making contact with Joshua. His posture loosened as he walked backward toward a chair in his office and sat down. After taking a seat he bent over, with his face to the ground and fingers locked into one another to help prevent his nerves from taking over.

"Are you OK?" Joshua asked after perceiving his breathing was slightly off.

"Yes." Dr. Trust said, while focusing on his catching breath.

Joshua placed his hand on Anthony's head and began to pray. "Father God . . ."

Dr. Trust reached his arm up and grabbed ahold of Joshua's wrist. His head slowly rose until his eyes were aligned perfectly with Joshua's. There was hellfire in his eyes, nothing but pure anger seething at Joshua.

"No!" he demanded. "I don't need the prayers of the righteous, No, not at all."

Joshua backed away as the atmosphere around him darkened. Joshua could see a cry for help in the fiery eyes of Dr. Trust and stood firm, planting his feet flat on the ground beneath him. "Satan I rebuke you in the name of Jesus." Joshua said.

Dr. Trust stood to his feet slowly and began marching forward, but with restraint as if something was holding him back.

"The blood of Jesus!" Joshua affirmed once more. "The blood, the blood, the blood of Jesus!" Joshua repeated until Dr. Trust became unemotional when his knees almost engraved into the ground. Joshua glided closer, placing his hand upon his head. "Jesus! Jesus! Jesus!"

Dr. Trust's stared intently into Joshua's eyes when a dark slithery voice climbed up from his belly, "He's mine!"

At 7:03 in the morning, Joseph immediately sprung upright in his bed covered in a cold sweat, breathing heavily as he lifted his shirt up over his head. Thoughts began pulsing through his mind intensely while he turned to the side of the bed, hanging his legs over the edge. Looking back at Sarah, he saw she was still sound asleep. He decided to move silently into the living room where he had always been able to easily concentrate. Joseph didn't have words to say, at least not to himself, but he did have questions to ask Dr. Trust. After twenty minutes of pacing back and forth across the room and wrestling with an interpretation for the dream, Joseph decided to make a phone call to the only person he knew that might have an answer.

An annoying ring was the sound Joseph heard for about thirty seconds until there's a voice on the other end.

"Hello?" Big Momma answered in an exhausted voice.

"Hi, Mae Nell, this is Joseph Johnson. I'm sorry it's so early in the morning..."

"That's quite all right. I'm up anyways baking some sweet potato pies." Big Momma interrupted, thinking Joseph finished his sentence because of how he ended it.

Joseph chuckled shortly before jumping straight to the point. "Well, if you aren't too busy, I would like to know if you could help me out with something."

"Yeah, come on over." Big Momma insisted. "You can help me finish baking and preparing the rest of these pies."

"Oh . . . well . . . um." Joseph stuttered not wanting to leave the comfort of his home. "OK, I'll be there as soon as I can."

Big Momma quietly laughed and insisted again. "Joseph, just come on by. Obviously you need some help and I need some as well, the pies aren't going to test themselves you know."

Joseph smiled, hanging up the phone, and then throwing on some clothes and jumping in the car. When he arrived at Big Momma's house, which happened to be only a five minute drive from his house, he thanked God for allowing safe travel as he walked to the door. Big Momma greeted him with open arms, gave him a great big hug, a kiss on the cheek and thanked him once again for just being himself. The two of them walked farther into the house and entered the kitchen to finish baking. About a half an hour went by and Joseph hadn't once mentioned the dream until there was a break in their conversation. But when he began to speak, Big Momma had something to say as well and incidentally cuts him off.

"So what was it you wanted help with?" Big Momma asked.

Joseph smiled after wondering if he would ever get a chance to find answers. "Well, I've been having these strange dreams ever since I passed out at the mall."

"Have you asked God the meaning of these dreams?"

"Yes, I have, but I've only received the meaning of only one part of the first dream. Now strangely enough, I just had a dream last night where I was watching what was happening, instead of me being involved."

"Well, what happened in this dream?" Big Momma curiously asked as she poured the pie mix into its shell.

"The dream started as Dr. Trust was talking to someone named Joshua about not being able to carry the burden of a doctor. Joshua did all he could to help, but even when it seemed that he was helping, Dr. Trust lost control of his self."

"Lost control how?"

"Possession." Joseph explained shortly. "Then Joshua says the blood of Jesus, trying to cast the demon out. Then he placed his hand atop Anthony's head, when all of a sudden this deep, dark voice told Joshua, 'He's mine.' And that's when I woke up and called you."

"Well, it seems like all we can do is pray for him. Things can be changed through the power of prayer." Big Momma affirmed. Joseph thought for sure she knew what could happen.

The two of them then said a powerful prayer that urged Big Momma into tears. Joseph even almost cried himself, but he took it upon himself to stand as strong as he could since Big Momma broke down the way she did. Joseph knelt down beside her and placed his hand on Big Momma's shoulders, "Are you doing all right?" he asked sincerely. "Is it your daughter?"

"Oh, I'm doing fine with that. Shawn was trying to play the part and make it seem like she was upset, but she just left town to go pick up something important."

"Oh, how are the boys taking her being gone?"

"Michael and Isaiah are doing OK, I can tell it affected them a lot because they are all very close to their mother." Big Momma said as she took the last of the pies out of the oven and placed them on the kitchen table so they could cool. "But that Shawn," Big Momma giggled. "That boy wanted to play a wise trick on us all."

"Well, that wasn't the funniest way of telling a joke."

Big Momma sighed. "Yeah, he isn't the funniest of the bunch. Poor boy has always been more of the serious type than a jokester."

After a few seconds of laughter, Joseph was the one to start the next conversation. "Big Momma," He said to get her attention. "I know this is out of nowhere, but what happened to your husband?"

"My husband, Theodore . . . ," she said, starting. "He passed away from prostate cancer in '92. Michael was just born, Isaiah was four and Shawn was six when it happened."

"Was he a great man?"

"He was a very great man. He was God fearing and he loved his family, friends, and church very much."

At the end of the sentence, I awoke from my sweet dreams and wandered into the kitchen because of the delicious aroma of those sweet potato pies my grandma would bake every year for

Thanksgiving. When I entered, I walked right to Big Momma, rubbing my eyes and looking up toward her.

"Grandma?" I said, attempting to retrieve her attention.

She looked down at me and smiled. "Michael, what are you doing out of bed?" she asked curiously.

"I woke up from my sleep because I could smell the pie," I said with a smile. "May I have a piece?"

"No, Michael, you're going to have to wait just like everyone else."

"OK," I said sadly.

"Hey Mike Mike." Joseph called me, giving me my nickname.

"Hi, JJ," I said.

This was the nickname I gave him after he told me his full name, Joseph Johnson. Big Momma walked over to one of the kitchen drawers and pulled out plastic wrap to cover the pies with.

"What have you been up to?" Joseph asked me.

When he asked that question, I looked at him with a strange look because at the time I didn't know what he meant by "been up to."

Joseph could tell I was confused. "I'm sorry. I mean, how are you doing?"

"I'm doing good. But my brothers keep telling me that my mom isn't coming back, but I told them that she'll be back real soon."

Immediately, Joseph and Big Momma looked at each other, as close to instant as you can get. Joseph didn't know what to say after I told him what my brothers said, and that moment he found out I obviously didn't know where my mother was. That's when Big Momma stepped in and told me that my mom was coming back. Isaiah and Shawn were trying to make me cry, and although it didn't work when they tried, I was very close to breaking down in tears.

"She'll be back as soon as she is able too. She forgot to bring one last thing from your home for the move."

"See?" I said exhaustibly. "I told them she was coming back. I knew she wasn't gone for good."

"All right Michael, it's time for you to head back to bed and get a little more rest."

"OK, Big Momma," I said, walking back to my room, but before I left the kitchen, I turned back to her. "Thank you."

"You're welcome," she said with a smile.

When I was completely out of the room, Big Momma and Joseph wrapped the last of the pies in plastic wrap and placed them all in the freezer except for two. One was for Joseph to take home and the other was a surprise for us after we ate dinner that night. All I know is my grandmother made the best sweet potato pies I have ever tasted, and I couldn't wait for everyone to try a slice on Thanksgiving Day.

Chapter Thirteen

All the Help You Need

1 Peter 5:8 (KJV)

Be sober, be vigilant; because your adversary the devil, as a roaring lion, walketh about, seeking whom he may devour.

November 25, 2004

When Thanksgiving Day finally arrived, I had become curious and was starting to understand—with the help of my grandma, Joseph, and Sarah—the idea of someone dying. Because I wanted to know so much about death, I wasn't able to focus my attention on eating the turkey and ham I had so long awaited for. The food was almost ready and the friends of my grandmother had already started to show up. First, at noon, it was Joseph and Sarah who had helped put the finishing touches on dinner, followed by Lanier "Pops" Bennett about an hour later. My grandmother had also invited two of her other new friends which had she made these past two months, Irene Tatum from church who had two sons of her own, and Nicole Thomas, who I didn't remember until she showed up at the door half an hour before we all sat down to eat.

When Nicole showed up, Pops was the first to stand out of his comfy chair to speak to this beautiful woman. I remember he stood up slowly with a mesmerized gaze upon his face and said, "Stenie." "Steh-nee" was how he pronounced it.

Nicole stopped and looked at Pops after realizing what name he called her. This was the first time I had ever seen Pops with such an attentive look on his face. He has always been so, what's the word I'm looking for? Oh, *comical*.

"What name did you just call me?" she asked.

"I'm sorry, it's just you look so familiar." Pops stated. "I used to know a young man by the name of Arthur Nelson. He was married to a young woman by the name of Stephanie Davis."

"That's my dad." she clarified.

"Stephanie must have been your mother then." Pops said.

Nicole was anxious to find out more. "Did you know them?"

"Yes, I did. Mae Nell and I both knew them."

"Knew them? We all grew up together." Big Momma said.

"I remember Stenie and Arthur had two of the best voices in the choir." Pops expressed before pausing shortly to take another look at Nicole. "Your mom and I were almost married at one point, but we ended up going our separate ways, that is until we were reunited almost thirty years later. She told me she had something she wanted me know and she wished she would have told me years ago. But unfortunately, because of time cut short, we never got a chance to sit down and talk. Maybe she wanted to let me know she had a daughter."

"Do you know what happened to my parents?"

Pops then came to the realization that Nicole never knew her parents. "Well, I do know that your father Arthur passed away after having a heart attack. How old are you by the way?"

"Twenty-seven."

"Well then, you couldn't have been more than a year old when your father passed."

"What happened with my mother?"

"I honestly don't know. But what I do know is she found me close to thirty years later and then after that she passed away as well. The cause was a heart attack, but even so she did ask me to help her look for something."

"Did she ever tell you what it was?"

"No, but at her funeral she did leave me this letter." Pops took a letter out of his wallet he had kept there for a couple of years and handed to Nicole to read.

Lanier,

I know we haven't talked in a while or even seen each other for that matter, but I need your help. I have been searching for something I sat down twenty-four years ago and have not yet found it. I know you haven't seen it before, but I know that when you see it, you'll know it was exactly what I was looking for. When you find it please show it the love that I never got the chance to do myself because of my foolish decisions when I was young. Thank you for always being there, you're a great friend.

Sincerely,

Stephanie

Everyone was engaged in another conversation after I came running and yelling to the table, interrupting the grown-ups and dragging Sam, one of Ms. Irene's sons, along with me. "Pops!" I yelled, grabbing everyone's attention. "Pops, you'll never believe it. Sam saw an angel like the ones you tell me about at church."

Everyone's attention then switched from their conversation to Sam and me, after hearing the word "angel."

"Where did you see the angel?" Pops directed the question to Sam.

"Don't listen to him. He didn't really see anything." Sam's brother, Julian, said.

Pops heard Julian, but ignored him. Instead, he directed another question to Sam. "How long ago did this happen?"

Sam thought about it for a few seconds, trying to recall the length of time it had been. "It was a few weeks ago."

"Did the angel speak to you at all?"

"No, I don't think he saw me."

"So the angel was a 'he'?" Pops recognized. "Do you remember how he looked?"

"All I could see was his white clothes because of the light surrounding him."

Pops, along with everyone else who had finally sat at the dinner table except for Sam and I, were all fascinated and wanted to hear more. "Why did the angel come? Were you in trouble?"

Sam looked over at Julian and saw that he didn't want to hear the story, so he shied away from the question. "Go ahead and tell us why the angel came. They won't believe it anyway." Julian said, knowing it would make his little brother happy.

I placed my hand on top of Sam's shoulder and encouraged him to continue. "I think he wants you to hurry because he's hungry," I said, shaking my head.

Everyone at the table laughed hysterically and then Sam spoke as the room became silent.

"The angel saved Julian when a car almost ran him over." When he said those words, the entire room was more than silent. I could almost hear each person's thoughts around the table as he continued. "I was getting a football out of the street for some kids and then Julian pushed me out the way of the car. I looked where he was, and that's when I saw Julian covered by the angel's arms, wings, and robe."

"See? See? I told you!" I uttered, as everyone was frozen by the hidden intensity in the story.

"Dinner is ready, and it is time to eat." Big Momma announced, as she and Sarah entered the dining room with all the different foods.

Everyone in the house was finally gathered around the table, sitting in their chairs with empty plates lying in front of them, and a spread of food you can't help but risk getting your hand smacked for attempting to eat before the family prayer. After everyone sat down Big Momma noticed I wasn't sitting down.

"Michael, come sit down at the table so we can pray."

I wasn't ready to stop talking about angels though, so I said, "No, I don't want to eat yet. I want to finish talking."

I remember Pops didn't say anything to me, he just gave me a look that made me know he was hungry and that we could talk later. That's when Big Momma got serious. "Michael, sit down and eat. You can talk about angels after dinner."

I loved and respected Big Momma, so I did as I was told, but since I was the last to sit down, Big Momma made me pray over everyone's dinner. But I was nervous. At that time, I had never prayed in front of this many people. The most I've prayed around was four; my grandmother, my mom, and my two brothers, but this seemed big to me. I felt like I was standing in front of an entire church as they all waited for me to pray.

"Can you please bow your heads and close your eyes?" I said to prep myself. "Dear God, I thank You for this food that Big Momma cooked for us and I thank You for bringing her friends over to eat with us. I ask that you keep sending your angels to protect us and that I one day would see an angel. In Jesus's name, Amen!"

When I finished praying, every immediately fixed their plates and dug into food. This was what started off as one of the most memorable Thanksgiving dinners I have ever been a part of.

While we were all enjoying our time together, Dr. Trust was spending his Thanksgiving dinner alone, after Joshua left back to Henderson, Nevada, to be with his church family. Some time passed, but it was only late afternoon. Dr. Trust had started to feel the loneliness sink into his mind. He didn't know what to do this year, because for all the years he's been back in Barstow, he had always spent Thanksgiving Day with us. Sitting in a room of silence, he became thirsty. He sprung quickly to his feet and went straight into the kitchen where he poured and drank a glass of water. The water was nowhere near able to quench his thirst, so he grabbed a couple of bottles of wine out of the cabinet, one for each hand.

Dr. Trust poured a glass of wine, followed by another, and another until the first bottle was gone. At this point he was still holding the second bottle of wine in his left hand while in a slump and just wanting to go to sleep. He sat in his very comfortable recliner chair and closed his eyes for just a second when he heard his name whispered. His eyes opened immediately and he looked around the room, but no one was there. He thought he was just hearing things until he heard the slithery whisper again.

"Anthony." the voice stretched his name.

This time Dr. Trust stood like Samson in the face of the lion, but with fire in his heart, ready for anything that was to come.

"C'mon! What are you waiting for?" Dr. Trust yelled, not knowing who or what he was screaming at.

After his demand, he saw the darkness in the corner behind his TV began to grow and creep toward him. His heart dropped to his belly as the courage he thought he had faded to the back of his mind. The voice became more vibrant, as it echoed off the four walls in to his ears.

"Anthony." the voice whispered again, as the darkness consumed the entire area around him, leaving only the small piece of carpet surrounding his feet. Dr. Trust thought to pace backward, shivering as an eclipsed figure walked out of the shadow toward him.

"What do you want?" Dr. Trust screamed.

The figure's hand reached out toward his face with its fingers spread, ready to reach around his head. "I already have what I want."

The figure didn't give any explanation of what it already had, but Dr. Trust knew at that moment when the words came out, they were directed toward him. Dr. Trust was immediately filled with fear and the thought of stepping back became an action. When he stepped back and his foot hit the floor, he saw that the darkness, which he would have stepped on, spread around his foot. *It either can't touch me or its toying with me*, Dr. Trust thought while continuing to walk backward. The figure moved swiftly toward Dr. Trust and stopped instantly when it was face-to-face with him.

"I'm not yours." Dr. Trust stressed with his eyes closed so he didn't look whatever it was in the eyes. "This isn't real. You're not really here." he affirmed.

The figure heard his words, and its presence immediately left. Dr. Trust opened his eyes only seconds after feeling the darkness flee and he exhaled in relief. The first thing he saw was the second bottle of wine still gripped in his hand. He stepped over to the kitchen counter, grabbed the bottle opener and took the cork out the bottle and started drinking again. After the first sip of the wine, Dr. Trust turned around, wiping down over his eyes, and was frozen in his steps. His eyes widened and he chucked the bottle forward after looking into the eyes of what he now thought was a demon. It had returned, but this time it was only inches from his face. The bottle went flying through it, causing it to vanish into the darkness.

The demon's eyes were fiery like the sun, and besides its eyes, its sharklike teeth were the only visible feature on its face.

"You are nothing!" The demon yelled, this time in a demonstrative voice.

Dr. Trust was in shock, but after a few seconds he was able to shake off a little of the fear, enough to sprint across the room toward a glass wall. The demon's eyes lit with hellfire as it slid across the ground, lying flat on its belly, toward him. The tail end of it looked shredded, just pure darkness spiraling in different directions as it moved. Dr. Trust was scared out his mind at this point.

With the demon speeding toward him, Dr. Trust slammed his eyes shut and called out without even thinking, "JESUS!" but the demon wasn't easily scared. It was a split second away from nearing him. And when it did, it stopped and slowly reached one of its hand up to touch his face. Dr. Trust opened his eyes and saw this malicious grin and needle-sharp fingers reaching for him, when out of nowhere, a bright light streamed through the air, slicing through the demon. On impact there was a loud explosion, like cannonballs erupting from volcanoes. Dr. Trust watched as the creature was slapped across the room, back into the darkened corner from where it came.

It happened so fast. Dr. Trust couldn't believe what had just transpired. One moment he felt as if he wanted to die, then he was staring death in the face, wanting to be saved. And when he did, he attested to have just seen . . . wings.

"An angel?" He spoke aloud trying to fathom if this was another dream or if it had become reality. Without any more thought, he sprinted into his room where he picked up the only thing he ever saw as real, a picture of him and his brother CJ. After staring at the picture and soaking it with tears for a few seconds, he saw his Bible underneath. This particular Bible was a reward to CJ because he was the first student in the Barstow Church of God in Christ Christian Day School that year, who memorized Psalms 119:1-20. When Dr. Trust saw the Bible, he reminisced about that day, seeing CJ stand in front of the entire church congregation and reciting verses 15 through 20.

¹⁵ *I will meditate in thy precepts, and have respect unto thy ways.*

¹⁶ *I will delight myself in thy statutes: I will not forget thy word.*

¹⁷ *Deal bountifully with thy servant, that I may live, and keep thy word.*

¹⁸ *Open thou mine eyes, that I may behold wondrous things out of thy law.*

¹⁹ *I am a stranger in the earth: hide not thy commandments from me.*

²⁰ *My soul breaketh for the longing that it hath unto thy judgments at all times.*

Anthony fell to his knees, and tears slowly flowed one by one down the sides of his cheeks. "I'm sorry, I'm sorry God," he cried until his tear ducts were dry, clutching the Bible in his arms close to his heart. The rest of that night Dr. Trust talked with God, thanking Him and discovering the still small voice of God speaking audibly to him.

During this happening, Robert and Malcolm went to visit Mrs. Robinson, Elise's grandmother. They had a great Thanksgiving dinner together, even Robert who was getting ready to take off and head home. He had to be at work within the next twelve hours so he wanted to get some rest before his shift.

Ever since Robert has had Malcolm around, people near or around him have seen how happy he's become. There was no more quietness. He was no longer always to himself and for the first time in nine years, he has allowed someone to be a part of his life; not even Demetri being his work partner was let in.

"Robert." Mrs. Robinson called.

Robert lifted his head to make eye contact. "Yes, ma'am?"

"How have things been taking care of Malcolm?"

"To my surprise everything has going great. I can honestly say that I have enjoyed having him around."

"Does he ask about Elise?"

"He does every day."

Mrs. Robinson was then filled with curiosity. "Does he wonder why she left?"

"Well, no, to be quite frank. He only asks about me and her when we were together. You know, when we were kids."

"Is he ever afraid that she won't come back home?"

"Mrs. Robinson, with all due respect, I have to work a double tomorrow so if we could continue this later I'd appreciate it."

"I'm sorry Robert. I'm just worried about him is all. But could you answer just one last question for me? I just want to be sure that he is capable of living with a stranger."

Robert was a little offended, who wouldn't be? But he understood where she was coming from. He knew that he had only known Malcolm for a little less than two months, but he had come to love him as his own.

"Well." He took a breath. "He did actually tell me that he wasn't scared because he knew that she wouldn't leave him with some she didn't trust." Robert stopped to think. "Do you have any idea of where she could be now?"

"I'm sorry I still don't. I wish I knew why she left that boy with you."

"We kind of got into a little argument right before she left. I hope I'm not the reason why she left." He took a pause after thinking she could be hurt somewhere. "I just hope she's OK."

"I'm sure she'll be just fine, and as far as you being the blame, I really don't believe that you are. She is a strong woman. I doubt something like an argument would be the cause."

"But I feel like I said some harsh things."

"Robert, please don't stress yourself out thinking that you are to blame. When she comes back, which I believe she will soon, I know that the things you said, did not stick with her. You should know that she's the kind of person that will forgive you at the moment the words are said."

"I—"

"Robert!" Malcolm said playfully after running to Robert, who was sitting at the kitchen table. "Can you tell me another story about you and my mom?"

"I don't know. I'm getting ready to leave for work."

"Pleeease!" Malcolm begged.

Robert grinned after seeing Malcolm's big cheesy smile. "I'll tell you what. I can start today but, we'll have to continue it another time."

"That's fine." Malcolm said excited. "But this time I want to hear one about something adventurous. I'm tired of hearing about love for now."

"OK. Give me a second though." Robert agreed with a chuckle and turned his attention back to Mrs. Robinson. "Thank you for this wonderful dinner. I'll come see you before I leave."

Mrs. Robinson smiled and said, "That's OK, we can say our goodbyes right now. An old lady has to turn in early."

After saying good night, Robert and Malcolm went into the guest room where Malcolm would sleep. Malcolm jumped into bed and pulled the blanket over himself. Once Malcolm was settled in, Robert started the story.

"All right, so an exciting story is what you want to hear?" Robert said while looking around the room to think. "OK, well, your mom and I loved to have fun. So on one Christmas Eve before we graduated, the two of us planned to go ice skating."

"But it doesn't snow in Barstow." Malcolm stated.

Robert laughed, "Yeah, I know, that's why me and your mom made plans to go somewhere that has an ice rink. Since I had a car, we set out late in the night before Christmas Eve, around 10:00 p.m. We said our prayers to ask God to watch over us as we were drove across the highway and went to a hotel in Los Angeles. When we finally arrived at the hotel about three hours later, we were exhausted and wanted to go straight to bed. As soon as we walked into our room, we dropped our bags in front of the door and flopped on the bed."

"You and my mom slept in the same bed?" Malcolm asked in the cute, I-don't-want-to-hear-that voice.

"No." Robert chuckled. "Actually, I let your mom sleep on the bed and being the gentleman I was, I slept on the floor with just a pillow and a blanket."

"Wait, so she bullied you onto the floor?"

Robert chuckled again and explained. "No, I told her she could have the bed because it wouldn't have been a good idea for us to sleep in the same bed and it was bad enough we were in the same room."

"Why?"

"Well . . ." Robert hesitated, wondering if he knew about, well you know, sex. Since he wasn't for sure, he stopped the story telling. "That's all for today."

"What!" Malcolm exclaimed. "I want to hear more."

"You will, but you have to wait until next time to hear the rest."

Malcolm sighed, "But you didn't tell half of it and it didn't even get good yet."

"It will, you just have to be patient and wait."

"If I have too." Malcolm whined and then laughed after finding something funny.

Robert finds his laughter interesting. "What's with the laughing?"

"I'll tell you next time."

The two of them laughed.

"All right." Robert said, patting Malcolm on his head and giving him a hug.

"I love you." Malcolm confessed, bringing an instant sensation of happiness to Robert.

Before Malcolm told him this, Robert hadn't known what it was like to hear those words since before he and Elise split. He wasn't sure how to respond so he just said how he felt.

"I love you, too."

Chapter Fourteen

Apologetics

Matthew 12:25 (KJV)

And Jesus knew their thoughts, and said unto them, Every kingdom divided against itself is brought to desolation; and every city or house divided against itself shall not stand.

November 28, 2004

Sunday afternoon immediately after church service, Big Momma, Shawn, Isaiah and I all left the house. When we got home, my brothers and I sat in front of the television to watch a football game while Big Momma strutted into the kitchen to get started on the night's dinner before the regulars show up. Well, just Pops. The only difference between this Sunday and every other Sunday at Big Momma's with Pops was we had what I like to call a special guest, Nicole. After finding out Pops and Big Momma knew her mom and dad, Nicole wanted to spend time with the two of them to learn more about her parents. She later found out that Big Momma felt like God brought the two of them together because of this very reason. Because of this special day, she wanted to be sure the food she cooked was some of her best work.

While we were waiting for Nicole to arrive with Pops, I decided to ask my oldest brother Shawn about angels. "Hey Shawn, do you think those stories about angels are true?"

"Yeah, I'm pretty sure," he said. "I don't think Pops would lie to either of us."

"Are you sure? Because I've never seen one and I would really like to."

"Well, maybe you will one of these days."

"Yeah, I hope so."

Twenty minutes later, the doorbell rang and Big Momma asked Shawn, shouting from the kitchen, to answer the door. Shawn decided it was a good idea not to answer because he felt he was too busy watching the game. Since Shawn decided to ignore our Big Momma, Isaiah sprung off the ground where he was sitting to open the door. It was Dr. Trust. Isaiah asked him in so he entered, saying thank you.

"Is Mae Nell home?" He asked politely.

Isaiah looked up at him and nodded. "Grandma!" he shouted. "Anthony is here!"

Big Momma just placed the last batch of seasoned and floured chicken in the vegetable oil skillet to fry, turning the fire under the chicken on low, when she heard Isaiah shout from the family room. She left the kitchen to greet Dr. Trust as if she wasn't surprised to see him. "Well, hello Anthony. How was your thanksgiving?"

"It was good."

Big Momma could hear the distress in voice his voice. "Don't lie to me now child. What's been going on with you?"

"Well . . . ," he started. "I believe interesting is the best way to describe Thanksgiving Day and every other day that has passed."

"Oh, and how so?"

"It's just that I think God is out to get me." Big Momma's expression changed out of curiosity and Dr. Trust smiled and explained himself. "Not in a bad way. It just seems that so many things are happening to and around me, and those things seem to all be trying to grab my attention."

"Well, you know you can't run from it."

"I know, it's just that the things that have been happening are . . . I guess, different."

"Well, what's different about them?"

"It all started with you earlier this year when you were transferred to being my patient after your regular doctor had to retire, then there were those two patients whom I had recently. One of them passed out at the mall, came here, and had a brain tumor."

"What's different about that?"

"He didn't have the tumor when he first arrived, and then it was full grown on his brain in less than six hours. Over the course of time he was there, the tumor began to drastically decrease in size. He didn't even know he had it until I addressed the issue to him."

"So what happened next?" Big Momma asked even though she knew.

"I released him, but I have him coming back tomorrow for a checkup. But that's only one of the strange things that happened. The other is one of the city paramedics who was on his way to work and was involved in a three-car crash, which landed him in a coma. I would think his wife would be devastated but somehow she is able to continue through life with a smile and few tears."

"It seems as though the love of God is healing them."

"How is it healing when so much pain was and is involved?"

Big Momma could sense there was something else bothering him so she politely brought it up. "Is there something else bothering you Anthony?"

Dr. Trust sat still without a peep until he realized that she might somehow know what's going on. "There was one other thing."

Big Momma's attention was grabbed and so was mine. I listen from around the corner as Dr. Trust continued.

"On Thanksgiving Day, I had a run in with something I thought to be a demon. I'm not too sure if it was exactly, but I am certain that it was not friendly."

"Was this a dream?" Big Momma asked.

"I only wish it was. I was at home drinking wine, probably more than I should have been, when something dark was in the midst. It was like a shadow of a wave surrounding me with sharp long teeth, jointed together forming a grin. It tried to attack me, but it never touched me. The funny thing about it though was it left when I said it wasn't there, but then when I least expected it, it was back and more furious than before. I ran across the room, and it followed until stopping inches away. From there it reached its hand toward me. I closed my eyes, trying to block out the fear and without even thinking I screamed, 'Jesus.' When out of nowhere a light shot from across the room and knocked the demon back into the corner from where it came."

Big Momma nodded as she pondered. "What do you think the light was?"

I don't know, Dr. Trust thought, *I was hoping that you could tell me.* "Maybe an angel, but that's the best guess I have. I thought I saw wings but I can't be too sure about it."

Big Momma nodded in agreement and then motioned Dr. Trust into the kitchen so she could finish up dinner. "So an angel huh?"

Big Momma mentioned while she turned over the last few pieces of chicken. "Do you still believe in angels?"

Dr. Trust hesitated. "Well, actually, I'm not sure. There were days when I know God is out there somewhere, but then there's always that doubt. I guess what I'm trying to say is, it's hard to believe in something you can't see, hear, touch, feel, or even smell for that matter. Too many bad and unforeseen events have happened, especially in these past months. It's just easier for me to stay true to myself than to hope for something good to happen."

Seconds before Big Momma opened her mouth to speak, the doorbell rang. This time Isaiah and I raced to the door with laughter written across our faces, competing to see who could reach the door first. Once near the door, Isaiah tripped over his feet which allowed me to reach the door first.

You know to this day, Isaiah wouldn't let me have this victory over him, he always said I tripped him and that's the only reason why I won.

When I opened the door, I saw Nicole standing to the left of Pops with a beautiful smile upon her face. Something good must have happened to or for her because according to Big Momma, Nicole hadn't had such an embracive smile on her face since the first day she spoke with her at the hospital.

"Mike, move to the side," Pops said. "I know you smell your grandmother's cooking sweeping through this house." Pops walked into the house and into the kitchen after seeing Big Momma talking to Dr. Trust.

Pops goes right up to Dr. Trust with a grin. "Have you wet the bed lately?"

Big Momma chuckled hysterically, but Dr. Trust only turned to Pops with a small bit of surprise wiped over his face. "It's been a long time Pops." Dr. Trust said. Big Momma left the two of them to talk and returned to the stove to get dinner finished up. I was still at the front door with Nicole as she laughed and smiled after seeing the look that was on my face.

"I knew it would happen. I just knew it!" I exclaimed.

"You knew what would happen?" she curiously asked. Before my next words, I had no idea that the woman I was looking at, wearing the astonishing white dress, was Nicole. She looked like her, but at the same time she looked so much different with her hair done beautifully and her pearly whites showing.

"I knew I would see an angel," I said with the biggest possible smile my little face could hold.

Nicole blushed a little after hearing those words. It had been a while since she's gotten a compliment from anyone, so for her to be mistaken as an angel must have felt great.

"Michael, it's me, Nicole."

I took a more detailed look at her, but still I thought she was very beautiful. She was definitely the first crush I had as a little boy and she was flattered. After she brought it to my attention and revealed that she wasn't an angel, I became embarrassed and apologized to her. Nicole bent down to my level and lifted my head back up, she told me that it was OK and that she really liked it. I didn't say a word, but she brought a smile to my face with her kindness. She grabbed ahold of my hand, and the two of us walked straight to the living room after I told her the food would be a little while longer.

Dr. Trust had looked up as we walked and sat in living room and was lost in his words trying to explain to Pops.

"What was that again?" Pops asked.

"Sorry I . . ." he hesitated.

"You were talking about what made you leave the church."

"Oh, that's right!" Dr. Trust said after being reminded where he left off. "It was a mixture of different things. There were so-called saints that were doing stuff the way they felt they should have been done instead of allowing things to be done the way God had given to the late Bishop Jones. No one seemed to care about the vision God gave Bishop so I decided to look for another church. And since I wasn't able to find one where I felt I needed to be there, I made the choice of doing things on my own."

Pops assessed Dr. Trust's words and to this day, I still don't know why he said what he did, but it changed Dr. Trust's look on everything.

"What does that have to do with price of rice in China?" When Pops said that, it was almost as if Dr. Trust's life was written across his forehead. Pops begin to ask him things which he had never told anyone. Dr. Trust didn't know how Pops knew what he was going through, but every single thing Pops mentioned, it happened in the past two months.

Big Momma called everyone to the kitchen table, but before Pops and Dr. Trust took a step, Pops mentioned one last thing, "God has wanted to help you for years. But He won't do that unless you call on Him for the help. The people in your life, the things you've seen, and those dreams you've been having were not by mistake. God has been blocking attacks by Satan in many different ways, and the only reason you haven't seen them is because you have been blinded by your own self." Pops placed his hand upon Dr. Trust's shoulder. "Just let go and let God. All you need to do is let go and let God."

Dr. Trust pondered on the words spoken as he and Pops walked to the kitchen table where everyone else was waiting. When Dr. Trust walked through the doorway of the dining room, the room was silent. He became uncomfortable with all the wandering eyes in the room that locked on him.

"Hi, everyone," he said as the speed of his heartbeat started to race nervously.

Everyone smiled and said hi except for Nicole; instead, she turned her head toward her plate. Big Momma saw and felt the tension between the two. "Nicole is everything OK?" she asked from across the table.

"Yes, everything is fine." she responded softly.

"OK child, I was just wondering."

Dr. Trust walked over to the only empty seat which was the last seat on the right, next to me. The entire time we were sitting together, all I wanted to do was talk about was everything I heard him tell Big Momma. I just had to know more. I was so fascinated with angels and demons at that time for some reason. I wanted to be Michael the archangel even though there was already one. But as soon as I opened my mouth, Big Momma told me I could talk to Dr. Trust after dinner, knowing what I wanted to talk about.

"But Big Momma?"

"But nothing, after everyone is finished eating then you can talk to him. You have to be considerate to others at all times no matter how much you might want to do something."

"Yes, ma'am," I said, hanging my head low.

"Anthony, would you please do the honor of praying for the food?" Big Momma asked.

Dr. Trust looked around the room, "Why me?" he asked with a chuckle.

"I figured since you hadn't been here for dinner in a while, you wouldn't mind. Besides, I want to make sure you're not out of practice," she said, out of the kindness of her heart.

Us three boys: Shawn, Isaiah, and I all giggled as he prepared to pray. "Um . . . ," he started. "Can you all please bow your heads and close your eyes." We all did and he began, "Dear God, we thank You for this food and for friends. We ask that You bless the hands that have prepared this food and that it's good for the soul. Thank You God, Amen!"

Everyone followed with 'Amen' and we dug into our plates that had already been prepared on the table by Big Momma. My brothers and I told Big Momma thank you for the food and Dr. Trust followed. "Yeah, thanks Mae Nell. This food is very delicious." Dr. Trust complemented after eating a spoonful of mashed potatoes and gravy.

"Yeah, very good, Mae Nell." Pops seconded. "You sure did put your foot in this meal." He complimented. "But it definitely seems like you washed them this time." he joked.

Everyone at the table laughed while enjoying their meals. "You aren't ever going to change, are you?" Big Momma asked.

"No, I don't plan on it. If there was one thing I asked the good Lord, it was to keep me well-balanced."

"But Pops, if you're well-balanced then how come in church, you're always leaning forward a little or your head is tilted back?" I asked.

"That's because he's always sleeping Mike." Shawn said.

Once again, we all laughed. This time when Dr. Trust laughed, he looked around the room and his eyes and Nicole's caught the same path. Nicole quickly looked away, not wanting to see him for some reason.

"I think the two of you need to talk." Big Momma recognized.

"I think so as well." Dr. Trust said, but Nicole disagreed. "I have nothing to talk to you about."

Dr. Trust stood to his feet and said to Nicole, "Could you please talk with me in the other room?"

Nicole looked at the end of the table where Big Momma was sitting, as if to ask if she should with her eyes. Big Momma nodded and said, "Go on, child. This food isn't going anywhere anytime soon. You can heat it up when you come back."

"Oh, it's going somewhere . . ." Pops added. "Right into my belly."

Nicole and Anthony then walked into the next room and sat down across from each other on the two maroon couches that were facing one another. When they left the kitchen table, I asked Big Momma, "How come Nicole gets to talk Dr. Trust but I can't?" But Big Momma just shook her head and laughed.

The silence was awkward with each of the seconds that passed, so Dr. Trust chose to break the silence and it became even more awkward, at least for Nicole. "Did I do something to you?" Dr. Trust asked politely. "If I did, then I'm very sorry."

Nicole sat quietly for a few seconds to think of how she would answer. "No, you didn't do anything." she whispered.

"Then how come you've been acting the way you have been whenever you see or talk to me?"

"What do you mean?"

"I mean, the longer Demetri is in the coma, the more I feel that you've grown a strong dislike for me. Take today for example. When

I walked into the dining room, as soon as you saw me your smile turned from bright to gray."

"At least it's not black." Nicole said, trying to lighten the mood.

"Nicole, I'm sorry, but I am doing everything in my power to help you and your husband. I didn't ask to be his doctor, God made it that way . . ." He paused, taking a quick breath. "And if I were you, I would put a little more faith in God and not in man since we can only do so much. I know I'm probably the last person you expect to give God credit, but it is true."

"It's not that I mean to make you feel that way." Nicole stopped to think. "You would see how it feels if you had someone close to you and you didn't know if you would ever hear their voice again."

Dr. Trust was shaken by her words, but he didn't show any extra emotion. Instead, he gave her advice that he wished he had used when his brother died. "Nicole, I urge you to be patient and let God handle it. If I remember correctly, all you have to do is ask and let God take care of the rest. Work your faith and your faith will build the work!"

Nicole's thoughts were frozen and had nothing to say except "Thank you!"

"You have to exult yourself in God. Once you do, there will be a major change in the things not seen."

Nicole walked over to Dr. Trust. "Thank you so much. I really needed to hear that. Can you please forgive me?"

"You never wronged me. I just want you to do the right thing so that you won't end up like I've been these past years. I used to be very close to God, never going against Him and His word. But there were a lot of things that happened in my life that I blamed God for, and that tore me apart. Don't ever do that to yourself because when things hurt, God is the only who will always be there for you to wipe your tear-stained eyes."

"Have you ever been told you were a wise man?"

"Yeah, actually, I have. But even the wise will lose sight on what's important for them if they allow it. I have some work to do on myself, and even though it will be a challenge, I know I will finish."

Nicole nodded understandably and then Dr. Trust said, "How about we go back in there with the others so we can eat?"

While Dr. Trust walked, thinking about the words that came from his mouth, he couldn't believe he still remembered all of it but he was glad. After they reached the dining room, Nicole and Dr. Trust sat back in the respective places silently.

"Are you two done arguing? Y'all ruined my dinner." Pops said.

"Sorry Pops." Dr. Trust replied.

"Honey, you don't have anything to apologize for. This plate scraper is already finishing his second plate." Big Momma said.

"Yeah, Pops, pretty soon one of those buttons on your shirt is going to fly across the room." Isaiah added. Even though this evening had the potential to end in disaster, God turned the line of cord leading to the dynamite into one of His beautiful works of art.

Chapter Fifteen

Uncovered

Ephesians 1:17-18 (KJV)

That the God of our Lord Jesus Christ, the Father of glory, may give unto you the spirit of wisdom and revelation in the knowledge of him: the eyes of your understanding being enlightened; that ye may know what is the hope of his calling.

December 3, 2004

Pops entered Big Momma's house with Nicole at his arm and collapsed slowly, falling on to his left side. Everyone was worried after seeing Pops hit the ground.

"Pops get up!" Shawn said.

"Yeah, the joke is over. Quit playing around." Isaiah reiterated.

Pops peeked through one of his eyes to see who all was around, but the only ones by his side were Shawn, Isaiah, and me. Everyone else inside the house was too busy laughing at Pops's mediocre acting job.

"Pops you really need to work on your falling technique," I said.

"Work on it?" he questioned. "I know you all aren't going to sit there and tell me that wasn't the best acting you've seen," he said, struggling to lift himself off the ground while proceeding to challenge us. "I bet none of you can do any better!"

"Mr. Bennett, next time you decide to fake a heart attack, don't look around to make sure everyone is watching first and then ease your way to the ground talking about, 'Lord don't take me now. I'm not ready to go.'" Joseph said.

When everyone was finished laughing at Pops for the birthday prank he tried to pull, mostly everyone went into the kitchen except for Pops, Joseph, Isaiah, and me. Isaiah and I were the two noisy ones in the house, so as soon as we heard Joseph say, "Pops, can you help me out with some strange dreams I've had?" we weren't going anywhere.

"Should I start with the first?"

"Yeah, I think so."

"Thanks by the way."

"You're welcome, just go ahead and fill me in and I'll see what the Lord gives me."

After Joseph told Pops the first dream he began to tell him the second dream, and Pops said, "One at a time young man, have you not read the story of Joseph in the book of Genesis? Pharaoh told Joseph one dream at a time."

Isaiah and I both giggled listening to Pops and Joseph. Joseph smiled and said, "My bad."

"So did God give you interpretation to any part of this dream?" Pops asked.

"No, but I figured out the fish represents the people in my life, the ones who stay to the end and the ones who won't."

"I see, said the blind man. You are right about that and the rest of the dream is plain to see, so let me start at the beginning. The reason you were looking out across the water is because you became curious after seeing the bright light. This light represented where you need to be going and swimming across the water wasn't just moving forward, but when you swam across the water was you taking a chance."

"So then there should be a road right?"

"The water is the road. It will be a long journey, causing you to become tired during the swim, and it will make you want to give up. But once you arrive, all that weight, tiredness, and pressure you felt will be lifted high off your shoulders." Pops stopped the interpretation and asked, "Did you get all that?"

Joseph was sitting next to Pops with a very concentrated face, hoping he didn't miss a word. "Yeah, so far."

"Good, good," Pop's said. "Now the silhouette of the man is you."

Joseph became confused. "How is that me if I was seeing it?" he asked.

"It's not you now, but it was after you had arrived. Hence, when you reached out to it, the light sort of engulfed your hand. There is something you do with your hands that God has given you as a gift and I'm sure you know what that is."

Instantly Joseph knew what it was, "My writing!" It all started making sense to him. The first dream and the second, they seemed to fit together, but how, Joseph didn't know. He decided to progress to the second dream, and Pops sat there listening as Joseph gave him every detail of it. When Joseph had finished, Pops began to interpret what God gave to him.

"As you should know now, this dream and the previous are one and the same, just different parts. The aquarium represented your mind and the reason you were standing outside of it was because you don't think like others."

"What about my mom?"

"She was standing with you representing something that can give you hope and reason to continue. Like when she said, 'You have to finish. No weapon formed against you shall prosper.' Then later goes on to say, 'Every task that is set before you, you will complete, but you must never give up.'"

"Thank you Pops, because I don't know how long it would have taken me to understand these dreams."

"It's a good thing God had you ask me then huh? You would have gotten to judgment day still wondering what in the world these dreams meant. But let me get to the part about the whale because that's my favorite. You see the whale is a task, and it obviously has to be moved for the whale to get out of your aquarium, or I should say your mind, so that all people can see. You don't know how you can do so, but that's when you remember about the man at the top balcony. This man is you once again, but he is the part of you that keeps you fighting to the finish."

"So he's the Holy Spirit?"

"Exactly!" Pops exclaimed. "So from there the Holy Spirit gives you the seed. The seed was nothing but faith. If faith can move mountains then I'm sure it can crumble a wall. Now when the faith flew toward the wall it didn't do anything right away, correct?"

"Yeah, that's right."

"That's because your faith will have to stand trial."

"What do you mean stand trial?"

"Your faith must stand the test of feeling defeated. Getting the whale out is going to take some time, so don't expect to hit a home run with every swing of the bat. You have to work your faith so your faith can work the situation."

Joseph leaned back on the couch. "That actually makes sense."

"It better had be. I don't think I would have to repeat myself." Pops joked. "Shoot, it made sense to me."

The two of them laughed together and then talked some more to get to know one another a little better. Everyone else in the house was having a great time together, but unfortunately we all had to go home and get some rest for the next day. Big Momma always told everyone before she went to bed, "I'll see you tomorrow if the Lord says the same."

Chapter Sixteen

Wish List

Psalms 33:21-22 (KJV)

For our heart shall rejoice in him, because we have
trusted in his holy name. Let thy mercy, O Lord,
be upon us, according as we hope in thee.

December 11, 2004

"Dear God," Malcolm started his prayer letter.

"Thank you for blessing me and my new friend Robert. I've always wanted a friend like him and I'm glad you sent him in my life. And God, I ask that you keep blessing me and Robert, and my grandma, and my mommy. Oh, and I know Christmas is coming up and I'll receive gifts, but the only thing I want more than anything is Robert to stay happy. You and I both know that he wasn't like this the first day I met him, but I'm glad he is cool like my mommy said. Oh, and if you could tell my mommy hi for me, I would appreciate it." Malcolm paused and smiled looking upward toward God and added, "I'm starting to miss her a lot too. But thank you God, Amen!"

After Malcolm finished his prayer, he hopped into the bed. Robert, who was kneeled down beside him, stood to his feet to tuck Malcolm under the covers.

"Hey Mac," Robert said to get Malcolm's attention. "I still have to finish that story about me and your mom." Malcolm turned to his side and propped his hand underneath his head to hold himself upright. "OK, so you remember the beginning of the story right?" Robert asked.

"Yes, I remember. You left off when the two of you drove down to LA and went to sleep."

"OK, so when we woke up that next morning we were freezing. The temperature outside had crept in to the window I had opened before I fell asleep. When your mom woke up she was a little upset with me. Not to the point where she didn't want to speak with me, more of a joking upset. After I got dressed in my blue denim jeans, white sweater, and black boots—topped off with a black bubble vest, beanie, white leather gloves, and a scarf—I walked to the car from the room so I can get the engine warmed up for your mom. She had no idea I went to do so because I told her I was just going to put the bags in trunk. The engine got warm fast so I sat inside the car for a few seconds to warm up my hands. I actually forgot cold air blows out the vents for a while before any hot air comes out, so I was even colder than before. I called your mom's phone to see when she was coming to the car but since she didn't answer, I took a jog to the room which was only forty feet from the car. When I arrived at the room, I stopped in front of the door to catch the little breath I had lost jogging and then opened the door. That moment was unforgettable. Your mom lit up the room brighter than any light was able to. Her white as snow smile widened in her winter wonderland outfit. At the time I didn't know if she was glowing, or it was because I've never seen anyone wear so much white."

"Did she like her outfit?" Malcolm asked. "Because every time she looks for clothes she can never make up her mind."

Robert laughed and answered. "Actually, you hit it right on the money. But even though she wasn't satisfied with what she was wearing, she was still content for the only time I can remember when it comes to clothes."

"What made her be content?"

Robert smiled after thinking how smart Malcolm was. "It was something about the color white that your mom loved. That was the last time I saw her wear white."

"Do you think it was because of me?" Malcolm asked as his innocent face overwhelmed Robert.

"Honestly, I don't think it was because of you. You were the outcome but not the cause."

"What do you mean?" Once again Robert was faced with bringing up sex and again, he didn't know how to explain it until Malcolm saw the look on his face and asked, "Do you know what sex is?"

Robert was caught off guard. *Did this boy really just ask me that?* he thought, and then asked himself, *Have I talked about it around him?*

"So do you? Because my mommy told me about it a few days before I stayed with you."

Robert was relieved but at the same time wondered why she told him or what she even said. "Yes, Malcolm, I know what sex is, but back to your mom. Having, well, you know sex, is no doubt why your mom stopped wearing white. She knew white to be the color of purity and felt that she wasn't able to wear it anymore."

"Why does she feel like that? Is it because she and you had sex?"

"Ummm . . ." was all he could squeeze out initially. "I think you should talk to your mom about that."

Malcolm nodded his head to signal for Robert to continue.

"OK, now back to the story. It's getting to the good part." Robert said, but Malcolm smirked and rolled his eyes, trying to say the story was boring. "Now when your mom and I walked back to the car, it was gone."

Malcolm's eyebrows rose. "Did it get stolen?"

"Actually, that's exactly what happened. When I went to get your mom, I left the car started and apparently someone took the car."

"Were you worried?"

"I was, but your mom just laughed, hoping to lighten the mood. But I couldn't believe I did that. Your mom told me not worry about because it was just a car and she was sure it would come back."

"Did my mom really believe that the car was going to come back on its own?"

"Yes, she did, as crazy it sounds. Your mom was, and I'm sure still is, an interesting character, but she was right. The person who stole the car ran the stop sign at the hotel exit and there just happened to be a police officer driving pass. The officer and his partner stopped the guy, found out the car wasn't his and brought it back to the hotel to see if the owner of the car was there."

"That's funny!" Malcolm exclaimed. "I want to be a police officer now."

"If you put your mind to it then you'll achieve it." Malcolm laughed hysterically, catching Robert's attention. "What's so funny?"

"You do know my mom real good."

Robert wondered what Malcolm meant until finally coming to the conclusion that the phrase he had just used was one that Elise had always said.

"So is that the end of the story?" Malcolm asked.

"It is if you don't want to hear the love part."

"You can tell me the love part now. I think the police will outweigh love anyways." Malcolm said with a content smile.

"Yeah, OK." Robert smiled as he continued. "After we got the car back, we went ahead with our plans and drove to the ice rink. We arrived and it was packed, to me anyway, but your mom insisted we had to go. Now mind you, your mom and I were just friends, but by this point in our lives we wanted to be together."

"How come you didn't then?"

"Honestly I don't know. We had done practically everything together up to this point and the thought of being together would have sealed the deal."

"My mom told me you were real good at skating, is that true?" Malcolm asked, changing the subject.

"Yeah, I was, but it's been so long that I don't know if I'll even be able to stand on ice skates anymore. I remember on that day I had to teach your mom how to skate because she was falling just about every time she stood on the ice."

"After you finish the story could you take me ice skating?"

Robert thought that would be fun for Malcolm, especially if he hadn't been in one before, so he decided to take him.

"Yeah, we can, but not right after this story."

"Could we go tomorrow?"

"I'll see if we can make the trip tomorrow since I don't have work. But you have to get to bed because if we do go we'll have to leave early in the morning."

"OK, I'll go to bed now." Malcolm said, ecstatic.

"All right, just be ready because I'll have to come and wake you up when I get up, OK?"

"Ok." Malcolm said as the big grin on his face depleted after finding out he had to wake up early.

After Malcolm fell sound asleep, Robert got things ready for their trip the next day. His mind started to wonder the moment he walked out the room into the kitchen, so he asked God a question that he has had on his mind since the day Elise broke his heart.

"God, why did she leave? The things she said back then and what I've learned just don't add up."

Throughout the night, up until he fell asleep, Robert was thinking about the night before he and Elise left for the ice rink. At the moment when they arrived inside the hotel room they were exhausted. They didn't have energy for anything except sleep. The two of them dropped their bags and laid in the bed; not too close though because neither one of them wanted to have sex before they were married. Plus, Robert was a young man and lying next to a beautiful young woman such as Elise would drive temptation straight to his heart and mind.

"Are you as tired as I am?" Elise asked Robert.

"Probably a little more." he responded as the sleep took over his eyelids.

"I'm happy we came . . ." Elise said before pausing to think. "You know, there is no one I'd rather be with than you."

Robert was happy to hear those words because he felt the same, but he thought expressing his feelings for her at that time might have led to cuddling, so he just smiled back.

"Is it hot in here or is it just me?" Elise asked.

"Yeah, it is a little."

Robert rose out of bed and cracked the window, allowing the cool breeze to burst through.

When he went back to bed, Elise seemed to be sound asleep. He thought to himself, *She must have been tired, or maybe it was the night air.* Five minutes passed by and Robert was at the brink of having the most wonderful dream of his life after the perfect drive down to the hotel. Then at that moment, Elise crept closer beside him to lie in the pocket between his chest and arm. Robert didn't know what to think. All he knew was he had never been this happy since before his parents had passed. Elise hadn't made a sound up until then, but Robert told me he would always cherish that moment when he swore he heard the last sound of her voice that night. But who wouldn't cherish it when the person they loved whispered in their ear, "I love you."

Chapter Seventeen

The Storm Is Over

Proverbs 12:25 (KJV)

*Heaviness in the heart of man maketh it
stoop: but a good word maketh it glad.*

Galatians 6:2 (KJV)

Bear ye one another's burdens, and so fulfill the law of Christ.

December 24, 2004

A t the church on the hill, the Barstow Church of God in Christ or COGIC, Joseph was leaving late after he chose to volunteer to help with the Christmas play the next afternoon when Dr. Trust called his name, "Joseph."

"Anthony!" Joseph exclaimed with his eyes squinted. "It's a surprise seeing you here. What brings you to this neck of the woods?"

"I was told by Mae Nell and Sarah that you would be up here. I spoke with Sarah earlier and she said the two of you were going to be at Mae Nell's. When I arrived there, I found out you were up here." Dr. Trust chuckled. "So it's been a while since we've spoken, well, I guess not too long."

"Yeah, it's only been a few weeks, but that seemed like forever after seeing you every day for about a month. But hey, I'm actually glad to see you. I've actually wanted to talk with you about something that I spoke with Mae Nell about recently."

"I've wanted to talk with you as well."

"I see you like to copy me." Joseph joked after becoming curious of what Dr. Trust wanted to converse about. "But what was it you needed to talk to me about?"

After hearing the go ahead, Dr. Trust jumped right into a question of his own.

"This might sound weird or it might not, but how are you able to keep so much faith in God? I just didn't understand how you could see the same cancer on your brain that I did and still trust that God would heal you."

Joseph chuckled at the thought. "Oh, trust me, it wasn't easy. After I found out, I couldn't believe it myself, but since I didn't feel any different than before, I figured out two things: it was there and you were seeing things, or there really was a tumor that grew but

God was already taking care of it. Like those times you asked me how I was feeling, the questions became more of a reassurance than anything else."

"But seeing you at the hospital made me angry with God. I just couldn't understand how He could love us so much that He would give his only son but would allow something like this to happen to someone who clearly has faith in Him no matter what."

"I cannot see, but I trust." Joseph whispered.

"Wait, what did you say? I know I've heard that somewhere before. Would you mind repeating it again?"

"I cannot see, but I trust. This was just something I picked up from my grandmother Louise Johnson when I was a little runt."

"Mrs. Johnson is your grandmother?" Dr. Trust asked after realizing where he had heard the phrase from.

"You know her?" Joseph asked.

"Yeah, well, I knew her when she was alive." Dr. Trust hesitated. "Mrs. Johnson and Mae Nell were the best of friends back before my family and I moved to Nevada. I wish I could've had another chance to see her before she passed away. She was a great woman of God, beautiful soul. She reminded me a lot of Mae Nell."

"I loved my grandmother very much. I would have loved for her to see how I've grown."

"I'm sure she would be proud to know you still walk beside God."

"Yeah." Joseph replied as a pleasant silence hovered in the atmosphere.

"So what was it that you wanted to talk with me about?" Dr. Trust asked breaking the silence.

"Oh, um," Joseph responded as he thought of a way to bring up Dr. Trust's brother being shot. "Mae Nell and I were talking a few weeks ago and she mentioned that your brother had passed on."

Dr. Trust was shaken after hearing the words being spoken, because like I stated before, he hadn't spoken of his brother's death since his parents moved him away.

"You don't have to talk about it if you don't want to. It's really none of my business anyway."

Dr. Trust shook his head side to side. "No, it's fine. I've needed to talk about this for a long time, but I've never felt comfortable enough to talk to anyone."

"You feel comfortable with me?" Joseph asked curiously.

"Yeah. Yes, surprisingly." he paused shortly. "It's weird though. I barely even know you but I feel like I've met you a long time before now."

"Man, Doc, you using pick-up lines on me now?" Joseph joked.

The two of them were filled with laughter for the next five seconds before Dr. Trust asked, "So you sure you want to hear about my brother?"

"Yeah, I would like to, but if you don't want to talk about, it's fine."

"No, it's OK." Dr. Trust said before reminiscing. "CJ and I were very close. We thought nothing could have torn us apart until his death happened. It's a sad thing though, knowing you could lose someone close to you without any warning."

"I know what you mean." Joseph said after thinking about his grandmother being gone.

"Yeah, but we have to go on right?" Joseph nodded in agreement as Dr. Trust continued. "When my brother was shot, we were walking from church one Sunday afternoon. We didn't live far either, only down the street from where Mae Nell's house was. As we approached Bishop Nathaniel Jones Jr. Way, the main street that brings you up here to the church and it's cross street, we heard people arguing outside of their house. I stopped walking and thought to myself, *But there was no way for us to go around to get to our house, and since we were almost home, I figured we might as well keep going.* When we were crossing in front of the house everything got quiet. I don't know what was said, but whatever it was made one of the men arguing reach behind his back, pull out a gun, and put the barrel on the other guy's forehead. The one with the gun yelled, 'I see you ain't got nothin' to say no more. Somebody was all talk huh.' The other guy didn't show much fear, but from the sweat that started rolling down the sides of the gun barrel from his forehead, you could tell he was a bit shaken up."

"Where were you and CJ at this point?"

"We were walking to the other side of the street at that time. But as soon as we started to cross, I looked back and saw the guy with the gun catch a look to the side of his face from somebody who had to have been against him as well. He came out of nowhere and the two of them ran in the direction of CJ and me."

"They must have thought he wouldn't have shot at them."

"Yeah, well, he did, and when the bullets went flying through the air, I reached around CJ so he wouldn't get hit, and we both crashed to the ground." Dr. Trust got choked up after thinking about the day, but cleared his throat and continued.

"Unfortunately though, he was still shot. The bullet pierced at an angle through his ribcage and punctured one of his lungs. When I finally noticed he was shot, I yelled as loud as I could for help, but everybody involved fled the scene. As I saw everyone run away, everything seemed to move in slow motion. I was able to see every detail on the three men involved, from the clothes to the tattoos that covered their arms and/or face, but because they never came around again they were never caught."

"Did anyone eventually help you?"

"Yeah, Big Momma Mae Nell Harris and her daughter Renee were the first people to arrive and be with me. They found me emotionally torn with tear-stained eyes, holding my brother in my arms with my head hung."

"Is that how you met her?"

"No. I knew Mae Nell before, but it was because of that day is when we became closer."

Another silence crept in the air, this time for a few seconds longer than before. When the silence was broken Dr. Trust told Joseph thank you, because before the two of them talked that day, he was afraid that he would be filled with the same emotions from the past. But the feelings never came back. He described it as a semi-truck being lifted off his chest after crushing every fiber of his being. When they finished talking Dr. Trust felt new. The only thing he felt he had to do was to get back in the good graces of God—but how?

Chapter Eighteen

The Gift of Giving

2 Corinthians 9:7 (KJV)

Every man according as he purposeth in his heart, so let him give; not grudgingly, or necessity: for God loveth a cheerful giver.

December 25, 2004

C hristmas morning had finally arrived and my brothers and I were very excited. Although our mom had seemed to pretty much disappear for a little while, I was still hopeful that she might arrive to be with the family before opening our gifts. Up until that morning I had failed to ask Shawn where exactly mom went since he seemed to be keeping it a secret from everybody. Since I was the first one awake that morning, I ran into the room where Shawn was sleeping and jumped on the bed while he was still sleep. He was a little upset at first because it was 8:01 in the morning, but when he realized what I was asking he calmed down.

"Where did mommy go? I've been leaving notes around for her and she hasn't read any of them."

Shawn rubbed his eyes and focused in on me since he just awoke. "Mike, don't worry. I'm sure mom will be home soon."

"But you were acting like she was gone for good."

"Well . . ." At that moment, I knew something was going on, and even though I was still a little sad because I hadn't seen her in a while I kept smiling, hoping to her soon. Isaiah woke up slowly as Shawn and I finished talking and came into the room where we were. Back then he never used to say much to anybody if they weren't family or a close friend.

A few minutes passed by and I left the room before Isaiah said something, "Are you going to get out of bed?" He asked Shawn.

"No." he joked. "I think I'll wait a little while."

All Isaiah did was nod his head and lie back down in the room, but before he was able to fall asleep, we could all smell Big Momma's I-want-seconds cooking coming from the kitchen. He and Shawn ran to the bathroom, brushed their teeth, and flew down the hall into the kitchen where there were six plates laid out for us all to eat before we opened presents.

"Are we having people over this morning?" Shawn asked Big Momma.

"Joseph and Sarah," I said, jumping interrupting their conversation. "They have presents under the tree too."

Big Momma just laughed. But it wasn't a normal laugh, it was silent. We all enjoyed watching her because her expression showed that she was laughing with her squinted eyes and mouth-widening smile as her body vibrated. But the funny thing about it was, there was no sound for a while. Shortly after she stopped laughing she called me nosey. I was confused though, because I didn't know what the word meant. So my response was, "I nose he?" Big Momma, Shawn, and Isaiah all laughed at me. It was the first time we had done so since we came to Barstow to visit Big Momma. Then the silence came as Big Momma finished fixing breakfast.

Only a few minutes passed before the doorbell rang and Isaiah and I laughed as we raced to open the door. This time he beat me but only by an inch. We opened the door and invited Joseph and Sarah inside so we all could eat. Everyone sat at the table except for Sarah because she was so eager to help Big Momma fix the plates. The food finally arrived, as one by one, the plates were sat atop the table. Pancakes, eggs, grits, sausages, two strips of bacon, and Ms. Butterworth's syrup to top off the pancakes, were on the mouthwatering plate.

"Wow!" was all Joseph could say.

"This looks and smells delicious Grandma." Shawn said as he attempted to take a bite of his pancakes.

"Shawn, could you do us the honor of blessing the food?" Big Momma asked while she and Sarah took a seat.

"Yes, ma'am."

Everyone bowed their heads as Shawn began to pray.

"God, we thank You for bringing us all here together once again. And God we thank You for this food that was prepared before us and for the hands You have blessed to do so. There are no other people I would want to spend this Christmas morning with than the ones You have placed here today. With that said we love You and ask for many more days like this. In Jesus's name we pray, thank you God, Amen!"

At that same moment, Robert and Malcolm were sitting down at Robert's house eating breakfast by themselves. Unfortunately, Robert had to go in to work that night, but the two of them made the best of it. Later that night Robert dropped Malcolm off at his grandmother's house and left for the hospital. He couldn't believe he hadn't been already, but he continued to walk anyway. His feet almost seemed to have a mind of their own while they were guiding him down the hall. His mind clearly wanted to leave, but his feet were taking a step at a time until he had finally arrived.

Upon entering the room he navigated, he stopped by the bedside and just looked.

"Thank you Demetri." Robert said, examining Demetri lying in the hospital bed, seeming so helpless. "I know I've never been the most faith having person you know, but I've been doing what I remember how to. I don't know what it is, if it's been Malcolm, you, or even Elise coming around again, but I have seen the difference in my faith drastically increase these past few months. Believe it or not, but I've even let people closer into my life for the first time in years, but hopefully we can chat a little more after you awake." Robert ended that sentence with a smile and once again thanked Demetri for the talks they did have when they had a chance. "I feel kind of ridiculous talking to you, but I hope you hear me regardless. The impact you made in my life was a lot more than I let on. You probably knew that of course, and I bet that's why you would constantly speak with me about believing again."

Robert's eyes began to water as he continued to reminisce. "I remember that time when we were on our way to the hospital and I didn't think we were going to be able to get that little girl there in time after she had been raped. All the cuts and bruises on her body, I couldn't even fathom the thought of someone wanting to do something like that to her. I drove as fast as I could but there was nothing to give me hope until you spoke, 'Don't worry, God's got it!' Those five words seemed so simple but made such an impact on me that day. It really took me back to before I lost my faith in God. I know now those words were a gift God gave to you to share with me."

At that time Nicole entered silently into the room and just listened to Robert speak to Demetri.

"There's one thing you need to do for yourself after you wake up. While I pray you could hear me right now, I just want you to love Nicole always. Never give up on the two of you no matter what may stand in your way. I haven't spoken to her personally, but I know for a fact that she's struggling right now."

A tear rolled gently down the right side of Nicole's face, then slowly one after another as she listened to Robert.

"She loves you, she truly loves you and I don't want what happened with Elise and me to happen to the two of you. You're on the right path of keeping God first so continue, and then she'll stay by your side because she is the one who God placed in your life to marry. Don't lose her."

"He won't!" Nicole exclaimed. Robert was slightly startled by her voice coming from behind him and caused him to turn around and face her. "I'm sorry I didn't mean to scare you."

"No . . . it's OK, don't even worry about it." He said with a smile.

"Is it possible?" Nicole asked.

"Is what possible?"

"I guess the real question is how do we stay in love that long?" Nicole paused for only a second before Robert answered.

"It's real simple, but seems impossible at the same time."

"Was it hard for you?"

Robert focused on her words trying to understand. "Was what hard?"

"Elise is it?" Robert nodded and she continued, "Was it hard to let her go?"

Robert was estranged to the question, but only because he wasn't sure of how to answer it. He shook his head slowly instead. "I haven't.

There has not been a time since we left one another when I haven't thought of her in some way. I think about her almost daily and when I don't think of her, I see her in a dream. Our break-up pieces were never put together, so I have no clue."

"What does that mean?" She curiously asked.

"It means that the things she said didn't add up, they made no sense. The person she is or was conflicted with why she ended it. Then Malcolm showed up, and that's when what she said started to seem true. Her telling me she was pregnant a week after graduation was when I thought for sure it was mine. I was happy and a little afraid, but then she told me that she couldn't be with me anymore. When she said that, I figured it wasn't mine since I couldn't think of any other reason why she would want to leave."

"So you don't know that Malcolm isn't yours?"

Robert shrugged his shoulders. "No, I don't."

A short stillness snuck in around them until Nicole spoke. "Maybe you should ask her."

"I would love to, but I can't. I haven't seen her since she left Malcolm at my house."

"Then when that time has come, talk to her."

Robert moved his head confusedly and said, "I have to get to work, but it was nice seeing you."

"Likewise." Nicole responded nicely, seeing that he clearly wanted to leave.

On his way out the room Robert told her, "Be patient. The best gift in life I believe, is love. When you have it, do not let it out of your sight for a second. Trust me, you don't want to lose it."

Robert nodded his head and exited the room. While walking down the hall he heard a still small voice whisper, "The gift of giving is found in many forms, but all come down to love." But Robert didn't look around for the voice; he just continued walking to the exit of the hospital. Nicole took heed to his words, and at the moment when she looked over at Demetri she saw his left pinky finger twitch.

Back at Big Momma's house, Dr. Trust had just stopped by to say hello. But the funny thing about stopping by to say hello to Big Momma, it always turned the hello into one big conversation.

"So how has things been for you this past week Anthony?"

"Everything has been, well, different. I can finally say and truly believe that God is the best father and friend anyone can have."

"Amen to that!" Joseph jumped in.

"So how have you been Mae Nell?" Dr. Trust asked. "It seems that every time I see you now we're talking about me."

"I'm blessed, Anthony. God has been good to me and I have no complaints."

"What about Renee? I haven't seen her around."

Joseph looked at Big Momma to see how she would react, but she stayed calm. But the funny thing about that was, at the moment she opened her mouth, there was a knock on the door. This time Isaiah and I began racing to the door but I stopped, almost as soon as we started. When Isaiah made it to the door, he grabbed the doorknob and looked back to see I was nowhere near. He opened the door anyway thinking I quit and his eyes widened. It was his best friend Corey from back home at the door. He hadn't seen Corey in years because he ended up in a group home for boys and girls after his parents died.

Behind Corey came our mom. I found out that morning she had driven up to Henderson, Nevada, and adopted Corey into the family and had to wait for some paperwork to finalize before she could bring him home. I was as happy as Isaiah was because Corey was like another older brother to me.

So all in all this was a great Christmas; old friends were reunited, Dr. Trust was no longer stuck in his selfish ways, and a young man by the name of Corey became my new older brother instead of pretend. God had performed many miracles that day, but those were only the beginning.

Chapter Nineteen

New Start

Acts 3:19-20 (KJV)

Repent ye therefore, and be converted, that your sins may be blotted out, when the times of refreshing shall come from the presence of the Lord. And he shall send Jesus Christ, which before was preached unto you.

December 31, 2004

When New Year's Eve finally came around, everyone was preparing for the New Year in their own special way. My entire family, consisting of Big Momma, my mom, Shawn, Isaiah, Corey, and myself were all getting ready for watch night service later to enter the New Year. Pops, Sarah, Joseph, and Nicole would all be there as well along with Ms. Irene and her two boys, Julian and Sam. My brothers and I normally didn't like going to church for New Year's because for one, every year we missed the countdown because they would lose track of time; and two, we wanted to stay home and have fun playing video games up until the New Year countdown began. But this year was different. Barstow COGIC was actually doing something to entertain not only the young children, but the entire church.

For some reason I couldn't tell you why there would be "A costume contest!" I exclaimed, wanting to do nothing else except have the best costume. The contest was to dress up like someone from the Bible and read your favorite scripture. At that moment, I knew who I wanted to be, and even though I didn't know what the prize could be, I was ready to take the church by storm with my costume.

"Who do you want to be?" my mom asked. As I thought of different great men from the Bible and even angels, I would always end up back at my original thought.

"John the Baptist." I told my mom with confidence. She looked at me wondering how she would be able to help me with my costume after trying to figure out how I would get a beard. But since my mom was, and still is, the best seamstress I've ever known or heard of, I already knew how she was going to help me. She ended up taking a piece of my lion costume from the Wizard of Oz since I couldn't fit it anymore, and created a mustache while I created the rest on my own.

None of my brothers decided to participate in the costume contest so I was the only one from the family, and it helped me feel that I had the best chance to win. I thought back to a past Halloween when Shawn grabbed a few body towels from the cabinet in the hall and made a robe out of them for fun. So that was my costume, towels. I used a total of three towels to make the costume. After I threw on a pair of shorts and a t-shirt just in case any unforeseen circumstances occurred, I wrapped one of the white towels around my waist. With the other two towels, I tucked each of them in the front and the back of the towel wrapped around my waist. After I finished putting my homemade costume together with paper clips, my mom brought my mustache. Then my costume was complete.

"Muahahaha." OK I didn't really do an evil laugh but I thought it would get a laugh out of you.

OK, so when we arrived at church that night, it was only an hour until the New Year began and the contest was underway. There was a mixture of kids and teenagers, and so far there was no one else whose costume was better than mine. Then it was my turn. I walked in from the side door leading from the fellowship hall into the sanctuary and everyone in the church was cheering for me as they did for the rest. I think they just thought I was just the cutest little thing. Either way, I'm sure they marveled at the creativity of my costume as I recited the scripture of my choice.

"John 3:16" I started, "For God so loved the world that He gave his only begotten Son, that whosoever believeth in Him should not perish but have everlasting life."

When I finished reading and left the stage, the last contestant entered. She was dressed as the Holy Spirit. Her costume was brilliant and had everyone in awe. She was wearing a white overthrow with a diced look on her hanging sleeves and white pants to match. Her face paint was so amazing that she looked as if she had a golden glow to her. I found out later that it was spots of glitter over the white face paint. There was also a wide hood covering her head. When she reached the middle of the stage where the microphone was standing she began to speak.

"Galatians 6:9-11. And let us not be weary in well doing: for in due season we will reap, if we faint not. As we have therefore opportunity, let us do good unto all men, especially unto them who are of the household of the faith. Ye see how large a letter I have written unto you with mine own hand."

A round of applause was given for the wonderful costume and the words from the Lord. All six contestants walked in front of the church for the entire congregation to see. Everyone in the church clapped for us young people voluntarily doing the Lord's work. As we all lined up side by side, the three judges had just put in their votes for most creative costume. When second and third place was announced I began thinking I wasn't going to win. The only person with a cool costume that hadn't been called besides me was Crystal, a.k.a. the Holy Spirit. At last the final results and winner of the contest was called.

"It was a hard choice to make, but the winners are Crystal and Michael." The first lady said, hesitating to call my name second.

A tie? I asked myself. I thought for sure that Crystal won hands down, but either way I was excited that I had won even if it was a tie. After the announcement, the head-usher of the church presented everyone with a prize. Place five through two all received their choice of a candy bar, while Crystal and I both received a giant milk chocolate Hershey's bar. When I walked back to my seat I had the biggest smile on my face for the rest of the night. As I took my seat, Bishop Nathaniel Jones Jr. approached the pulpit ready to preach with a hopeful smile on his face and only twenty minutes left until the New Year.

"Since I only have about twenty minutes left before we head into the New Year, I'll try my best not preach into it this time around. The message the Lord has given to me to give to you is titled 'The Blind Walk.' You see, we are all on a blind walk with God, but the fact of the matter is, we don't know how to walk the walk that is intended."

Bishop Jones proceeded to walk to the left of the pulpit looking out into the pews and holding the cordless microphone in his hand.

"Right now I'm going to tell you a story, and I want you to listen very carefully and understand what God is trying to tell you. The story starts with a young man who was raised in the church, and became a great preacher. He was invited places, continued to carry on God's work, and in turn received a big name for himself over time. But in the midst of all of this fame, he lost touch with what brought him to where he was—his relationship with God. It began to dwindle to the point where he no longer felt that he needed to consult with God, so he started doing things his own way.

One night as he lay to bed, he found himself in a white space, a room of some sort with no walls or ceiling but a floor. He didn't know where he was or why he was there until a man came to meet him. He knew right away who it was, the man who came to meet him was Jesus, and they began to walk silently. As they were walking, the man had so many questions and thoughts racing through his head but he didn't speak. Then he began to see a figure in the distance coming toward them, but he can't quite make out what it was. As they get closer, he could make out the silhouette of the figure to be a person, but still wasn't able to quite make out who it was. They got closer and closer, and the man could see that this person was walking very gracefully with a fresh white suit on and a nice fresh haircut and he thought to himself, *This guy looks familiar . . .* But still he couldn't make out who he was. They proceeded closer, and the man couldn't take it anymore. Hearing his own and Jesus's footsteps touching the ground with each step echoing in his ear, he turned and asked Jesus, 'Who is this man?' But Jesus didn't say a word, so the man asked Jesus again, 'Jesus, who is this man standing before you and me? He looks very familiar but I have no idea who he is.' Jesus turned to him and said, 'This is the man I intended you to be . . .' The man immediately snapped out of what he thought to be a trance. But it was a vision that seemed to last hours, but in reality went by in a flash of a minute."

With that said the story was over. The entire church was at a standstill. I'm sure everyone in the church was thinking the same one word I was, *Wow!* Bishop then looked at the clock and saw there was only one minute to spare, and so he ended with this

"Don't let this world keep you from Salvation. Graduate this life, and be the person that God intended you to be. God bless!"

Thirty minutes earlier at 11:29 p.m., Dr. Trust was leaving the hospital after saving a patient who was brought there by Robert. While driving home, he began thinking about everything God has done to help him from his past. In the midst of his thinking, he once again felt a strange presence around him. As he continued on home he started to pray.

"Father God, whatever this is I can feel around me, I need you to get rid of it. Nothing has felt like this all day around me, so why did it choose now? Either way God, I need your protection. After what I experienced the last time I know I cannot do this on my own. Send your angels to be with me, in Jesus's name, Amen."

When Dr. Trust finished praying he still felt a little uneasy, but by the time he arrived at home there was nothing bothering him, he felt at peace. Dr. Trust was at the front of his house positioning his car to back into the driveway. And when he glanced in the mirror to see what angle he needed to take, he turned his upper body around to get a better view of where he was going.

Out of nowhere the same demon from before appeared in the backseat, staring face-to-face with him. He was shock, jumping back and hitting the horn on his steering wheel; he placed his car in park and exited quickly without closing the door.

"What do you want?" he asked while sidestepping to the front door of his house and keeping his eyes on the demon. At his arrival to the door, he glanced behind him swiftly just to see where the door handle was, but when he looked back in the car the creature was no longer there. Dr. Trust walked back to the car to observe it and there was really nothing there. He took the key out of the ignition and walked to enter his house. Once inside the house he looked around and everything seemed fine. He thought to himself, *Am I seeing things because of the incident before*? but he believed he was wide awake.

Since the house was silent Dr. Trust entered further with no worry. He closed the door and locked it behind him, but after turning to the right he noticed the ceiling corner was full of darkness. It seemed to be just the light this time. So after building up enough courage, Dr. Trust proceeded with caution toward the corner. Once underneath, he pulled his cell phone out of his pocket and shone the phone's flash light toward the darkness. Everything was normal when he did so, until he heard a slithery laugh coming from that exact corner. Dr. Trust was petrified as chills shot through his spine. The creature then extended out of the ceiling corner with its grimacing smile and sharp fingertip hands reaching toward his face. Right before it touched his face, Dr. Trust woke up in his office chair at work with his head and body covered in a cold sweat. He was breathing heavily as the shock from the dream carried over as he awoke.

"Jesus." he whispered, wanting someone to talk to. Since Joshua left town, Dr. Trust had been at home alone and hasn't had anyone he could trust besides Joseph and Big Momma. Because he knew they were in church he decided to walk to Demetri's room to speak with him. When he reached the room he saw Nicole sitting at Demetri's bedside.

"Excuse me Mrs. Thomas," he said after seeing her next to her husband and being taken by surprise.

Nicole turned and saw him standing in the doorway.

"Hi, Dr. Trust. How long have you been standing there?"

"Oh, um, I just arrived and saw you sitting there and I wanted to see if we could talk."

"No, I don't mind at all. I was just here speaking with God about Demetri, wondering if He could possibly give me a sign or something."

"So the waiting is still weighing on you huh?"

Nicole nodded. "Yes, it is, but I am doing a lot better with it."

"That's good to know. The last thing you or Demetri need right now is for you to worry yourself."

"Yeah, I know." She agreed. "So are there any updates on Demetri's status?"

"Well, actually, that's what I came to the room to talk to you about. On Christmas Day when I left the hospital, something happened." Dr. Trust pulled out the chart at the end of the bed and explained. "You see here, on October 20, his heartbeat pattern changed drastically. This has happened on a couple of other occasions as well." He dragged his finger across Demetri's heartbeat on the chart. "November 24 was the other time it happened. As you can see right here, there's a quick spike in his pulse."

"What does that mean?"

"Honestly I don't know, I can only guess he's dreaming, which is very likely."

After hearing the uncertainty in his voice Nicole asked curiously, "Do you think it could be something else?"

"If it is something else I have no idea of what it could be, his vitals seem normal so besides that, there isn't anything wrong with him except for the fact he's in a coma."

"There has to be something you can do?"

"I'm afraid not Mrs. Thomas."

"Please, call me Nicole." She offered.

"OK, Nicole. Neither I nor anyone I have contacted about this situation has seen anything like it. Each spike was sporadic, jumping so far only twice, and honestly at this point all we can do is trust in and wait on God." A short silence rose before he continued, changing the subject. "The New Year is only five minutes away. You should get ready to celebrate. And for you to know, over in the hospital cafeteria are some of the patient's family members who are getting ready to watch the ball drop on television. Feel free to join them if you'd like." Dr. Trust ended with a smile before leaving the room. For the next five minutes Nicole just sat in silence alone, thinking about the last moment the two of them had together.

"If I would have held you for a few seconds longer then maybe you wouldn't be in here. I know I can't change what happened, but I'm upset with myself knowing that I could have prevented this. I'm sorry!"

"It's OK." a heavenly voice whispered very quietly; barely able to hear.

Even though it was very light, Nicole still heard the voice. It seemed so familiar but she couldn't figure out who it was. *Demetri*, she thought until seeing the reality that he was sleeping softly in a coma. Nicole didn't know what to think so she waited, holding Demetri's left hand with hers until the New Year began.

Two hours earlier, before Robert arrived at work, he had just gotten Malcolm's things packed and ready to drop him off at Mrs. Robinson's house.

"Malcolm, did you remember your toothbrush?" Robert asked.

"Yes, I did!" he yelled from the back room.

"OK, well, it's time to go, and don't forget your jacket."

"OK, I'm coming." Malcolm said.

When Malcolm made it to the living room, Robert knelt to be eye level with him. "As soon as I'm off work in the morning I'll come by and pick you up, OK?"

"How come you can't stay with me for the New Year?" Malcolm asked while rocking side to side with his face hung low.

"I would love to, but unfortunately lives have to be saved and I'm one of the people in this city that God has . . ." Robert hesitated before finishing his sentence. It brought a smile to his face to see that God has in fact still chosen him to do good in the world even though he's tried to keep people out of his life. ". . . chosen to do so."

"OK." Malcolm whined understandably.

Robert hugged Malcolm and told him there will be many other New Year's they would spend together, and then they exited the house. As soon as Robert opened the door, surprisingly enough, Elise was walking toward the house and was only a few feet from the doorsteps.

Malcolm ran to her; to give his mommy a great big hug. "I missed you so much!" Elise said.

Robert on the other hand couldn't believe she was standing only a few feet from him. He also couldn't help but remember the last time the two of them had spoken; we all remember how that turned out.

When Elise and Malcolm stopped hugging they both turned to Robert. "Hi, Robert," Elise said hoping to hear a response. But he wasn't sure what to say back. His emotions were all mixed up after reminiscing about the past and then seeing her standing in front of him. "I know you're probably still upset with me for a number of things, so first let me say I'm sorry. I didn't—"

"Just stop right there." Robert interrupted as kind as he could.

"But—"

"Just stop please." He begged in a soft tone once again, interrupting her. "There's no need for this."

Elise was then confused after those words rolled from his tongue. Even though he didn't seem to be upset at her, with the choice of words he used, Robert could have been either forgiving her or quite the opposite.

"I just need you answer me. Why?"

"Why what?"

"Why did you leave your son with me? There could not have been anything that important that you had to basically dump Malcolm with me or with anyone for that matter. So can you please enlighten me on what's going on? And no beating around the bush either."

"My plan originally was not to leave Malcolm with you the way I did. I wanted more time to sit down and actually play catch with you. But while I was on my way here I had to change my flight."

"Where did you go and why didn't you just take Malcolm with you?"

"I went to Michigan and I barely had enough money to buy myself a ticket. I didn't bring Malcolm because of that. The best thing for me to do was leave him with someone I knew, and since my grandmother wasn't able to, I turned to the only person I knew could."

"Yeah, I spoke with her over the phone and in person. She's the one who has been keeping Malcolm while I was at work. And I know I'm asking a lot of questions, but what were you doing in Michigan all this time?"

"Ashley called me. Apparently my mom wasn't doing well with her sickness and it took a turn for the worse so I had to rush out there."

"Is she OK now?"

"She's doing better. She got sick at the time Malcolm was born. He still hasn't had a chance to meet her yet, but hopefully I can take him out there soon so they can finally meet."

"That would be nice," Robert said. "Well, I hate to rush out of here, but I have to drop Malcolm over your grandmother's house because I have work in about an hour."

"Would you mind if I rode with you? I took a taxi here from the airport and I was planning on stopping by her house anyway before I went back home."

"No, I don't mind at all."

Once the three of them were settled in the car, Malcolm and Elise in the backseat, they were on their way. Mrs. Robinson's house was only fifteen minutes from Robert's, but the time seemed to drag along with the awkwardness in the midst. Robert could see in Elise's eyes that there was something else she needed to say, and by that time, five minutes of silence had passed by and Malcolm had fallen asleep.

"Are you OK?" he asked.

"Yeah, I'm fine. Why do you ask?"

"When you're nervous you look around and your eyes have a subtle twitch about them."

Elise looked down to see Malcolm was sleeping peacefully and took a deep breath. "Robert, there is something I need to tell you."

Robert glanced in the rearview mirror. "What is it?"

"Malcolm is your son."

Robert was caught off guard by the straight-to-the-point attitude Elise has always had and a shock of nerves that shot through his body.

"Huh?"

"I said Malcolm is your son." Elise said slower than the time before.

"Are you sure? I mean how do you know?"

"Maybe we should talk about this later." Elise suggested.

"No, we need to talk about this now. I can't go to work and have to wonder if this true or not. I mean, there was a part of me saying that he is, but I didn't believe it. I need to know now, so how is he my son when you said he wasn't those years ago?"

"Because . . ." Elise hesitated. "I've never been with any other man besides you."

Robert was shocked but relieved at the same time to know the two of them had only been with each other. "You've been alone all these years?"

"No, I've had boyfriends. I just haven't slept with anyone except for you."

Robert was once again caught off guard and so he asked the first thing that came to mind. "Are you sure?"

"Yes, I'm sure." Elise said with a slight smile and shimmer in her eyes from the tears that built up.

Finally at Mrs. Robinson's house, Robert parked by the side of the curb, turned the car ignition off and turned around to look at Elise. "Why did you tell me you were pregnant with someone else's child?"

"I didn't. All I said was he wasn't yours because I wanted you to follow your career plan and not have to worry about taking care of me or the baby. I knew you would have dedicated yourself to us and would have ended up doing something you never wanted to do if I hadn't."

"But Elise, how do you know I wouldn't have chased what I wanted."

"I don't."

"Exactly, because if I want something bad enough, I'll go get it or wait if I have too like I did with you!" Elise looked up at Robert from the ground and was surprised to hear what he had just said.

"You waited for me?"

Robert couldn't believe it himself. He knew he still wanted to be with her but he didn't want to say anything because he was still afraid. "Look, I have to go to work," he said very uncertainly as he exited the car and took Malcolm out to lay him over his shoulder. Elise exited after and they walked toward the front door.

"Are you mad at me?" Elise asked half a second behind Robert.

"No, I'm not mad, just disappointed. I could have taken care of you and Malcolm and still chased my career. That's what a man does. He's supposed to work to provide for his family. And even though we weren't married, we would have been by now."

"I'm sorry Robert," Elise said after remembering the box with the ring he dropped the last night they saw each other.

But Robert didn't say anything back. He just woke Malcolm up and set him down when in front of the door. "Little Mac, I'll be back as soon as I can, OK?"

Malcolm nodded his sleepy head and hugged Robert tightly around the neck for a few seconds. "You be good to your mom now, I love you."

"I love you too, Robert."

"I'll talk to Malcolm while you're away," Elise said, looking Robert in the eyes sincerely. "And we'll both see you when you come back."

"Look Elise," Robert started, trying to prepare for what he was about to say next. "What's done is done and it can't be changed." Elise looked at the ground, preparing for what she knew would come. "But I want to build us back together. I know, I know, it's going to take some time but I think it's in the best interest of all of us."

"I don't know Robert. Look what happened last time."

"But this isn't last time. All I know is I've been waiting for this moment for what seemed like an eternity, and I'm not going to lose you again." Elise shrugged her shoulders and stayed quiet, so he continued. "Elise, I'm not saying we jump the gun and get back into a relationship and get married. I'm just saying let's start over as friends. There has been a lot of time that passed and I know there's more to each of us than we used to know. So if you're willing, I want you to know that I don't have a doubt in my mind, no matter what happened all those years ago, that I want you back."

But she still didn't say anything. Robert could see that she was thinking so he turned and walked to his car, but when he was nearing his car Elise yelled out, "I would like that."

"Excuse me?" he asked, just to make sure he wasn't hearing things.

Elise walked toward Robert and met him where he was standing, reaching out to him to wrap her arms around him tightly. "I love you Robert, and thank you for being the same person I fell in love with."

Robert was happy. Well, actually, he was more than happy, but he didn't want to overdo anything and tell her he loved her back for reasons he wouldn't say. "Well, I guess we'll talk later?"

Robert began to pull away, and Elise stood on her toes and kissed him on the cheek. Malcolm and Elise said their goodbyes as he leaves for work.

At 11:40 p.m., ten minutes after he arrived at work, he and Demetri's replacement, Timothy, were prepared for a busy night. Only a few minutes went by before their first alert came, and they entered the ambulance to rush a few blocks over where a fire had started. When they arrived, the surrounding houses were all evacuated and the pedestrians gathered behind a barricaded area. Police officers were keeping people behind the barricade as the firemen attempted to control and eventually put out the fire. A news chopper was circling the sky, recording as the flames of the fire waved and sparks flew in various directions. Robert and Timothy were the first on scene besides two fire trucks, followed by various emergency vehicles, as the fire seemed to grow with each second that passed. When he heard people screaming from inside the house, Robert looked around and saw that none of the firemen could hear the screams so he alerted one of them.

"There is someone still inside that house."

"We already evacuated everyone out of the house, there's no one left."

"You're telling me you don't hear the scream?"

"I'm telling you, we got everyone out the house. We would have known if someone was still in there."

Robert became frustrated trying to convince the fireman otherwise, so he decided to take matters into his own hands without thinking he could be burned. Timothy was the only one who saw Robert enter the burning two story house and told the firemen what happened.

Even though he was using his jacket to cover his mouth after he entered, Robert was still breathing in smoke and coughing as the heat began to quickly take a toll on him. The screams for help then became more apparent as he walked up the stairs to the top floor.

"Hello, is anybody in here?" he asked, not sure if he really heard a scream after a couple of calls.

In the midst of this battle against fire, Robert began to wonder why he ran in the house with no protection like a mad man, but regardless of the thought, he knew he had to do something about it. While walking through the fiery hallway, Robert heard the calls for help again coming from a nearby room to the left of him. The room was blocked off by pieces of the roof that had fallen, so he entered the room next to it and climbed out the window to a lower part of the roof. Once outside the window of the room where the screams were coming from, he broke the window and climbed through it with no problem.

He looked around the room but didn't see anyone. No one was under the bed or crouched in a corner, but then he opened the closet sliding door and found a little girl, around fifteen years of age, wrapped in blankets.

"Are you alone?" Robert asked the girl.

"Someone wrapped me in these blankets," she said, shaking her head no. Once she told him there was someone else, he started to question if the firemen had actually entered the house. Either way Robert knew he had to get the girl out.

"Wait here!" Robert told the girl while he walked to the blocked door and started kicking the fallen ceiling pieces until it was clear. As soon as it was clear, Robert lifted her in his arms, seeing it would be easier to carry her through the hall and down the stairs this way. At the bottom of the stairs Robert was almost unable to see, but he continued as best he could. As the two of them approached the door, a small piece of the ceiling fell and hit Robert on the top of the head, knocking him down. The little girl knelt and started shaking him for about thirty seconds, but she began to cry when there was no response.

At that moment, a man knelt by Robert's side and said, "Robert, stand up. You have to get up." Robert listened but couldn't see anything. He knew someone was there because he felt a man's hand grab ahold his. "The Lord is your strength and refuge when you are in trouble," the man spoke.

Robert's eyes slowly began to open, wide enough to see and keep the smoke out. The little girl saw Robert's eyes opening as he slowly rose to his feet and grabbed his hand. He looked around for the man who was talking but saw no one.

"Demetri?" he asked himself after thinking of how the man's voice sounded. When he saw no one around he thought of nothing except for getting the girl out the house and he did so. He and the girl were safe as they walked out the house together and into the arms of the firemen and paramedics on scene.

"There's someone else in the house!" Robert told one of the firemen, but the two of them both knew it was too late to go in. Almost a half an hour into the New Year and the fire was out. When there were no more flames and debris falling from the air, the firemen were all done searching the house for any possible bodies that could have been trapped in the house. Robert had come back to the scene after he and Timothy had dropped the girl off at the hospital to see if anyone had been found.

"Did you find anyone?" Robert asked the chief fireman.

"No, there's no trace of anyone who got caught in the fire. I'd say you did good, son. It takes a lot of love to risk your life for someone who you weren't even sure was there at all," the chief stated.

Robert nodded as he and the fire chief walked away, wondering where the man was. Once Robert arrived at his ambulance he called Mrs. Robinson's house to talk with Elise, but Malcolm answered the phone and told him she left the house a few minutes ago. Robert couldn't help but think that she left Malcolm again but had hoped she would be at the house when he went back. He walked to the back of the ambulance to make sure the door was closed and when he did, he saw Elise standing behind the barricade. After walking to her quickly, Robert gave her a tight hug and whispered in her ear, "and I love you."

Now into the New Year, everything had started off going great aside from the fire that burned the house down, but God took care of that. No one was seriously injured except for Robert taking a hit to the top of the head by the ceiling. And although he still struggled for a short while, he and Elise did begin to build their relationship back slowly but faster than either of them thought. This was a prime example of God choosing two people for each other. When they first told me a little of how they met was the moment I had started wanting to fall in love.

Dr. Anthony Trust even became a new man. A New Year for most people usually meant a fresh start or a clean slate. But for him, the end of the year 2004 for became more than just a clean slate; it became the beginning of the renewing of his relationship with God.

Joseph and Sarah were soon expecting to add a new member to their family and they couldn't have been happier. Sarah's business, Generational Beauty, was doing very good, attracting customers from different cities and states when they were passing through Barstow along their way to Las Vegas or Los Angeles. Joseph went ahead and started to follow the dreams God had given him and started writing even more than he had. His first book was titled, *Don't Stop, Keep Moving*, and was almost finished; drawing the attention of publishers from across the country wanting to publish his book. What more could he want?

Along with Joseph and Sarah, Nicole and Demetri were also expecting to add a new member to their family in 2005. Nicole was still struggling a little without Demetri, but after becoming closer with Big Momma and Pops, her waiting became a little easier. As far as Demetri, he was still in a coma at the beginning of the New Year, and Nicole stayed hopeful that he would wake before their child was born.

And as for my brothers and I, we all had a little bit of growing up to do before we had to face life's more challenging obstacles. After gaining another family member, life became much more exciting. All we had left to do now was to wait for the years to pass by. As we grew older, more miracles happened along with some tragedies and . . . well, I probably shouldn't tell you yet, and plus, I think that's a story I'll have to tell you another time.

About the Author

 I've been writing since I was in fourth grade as far as I can remember. And throughout the past thirteen years, I have honed my writing skills by paying attention in school and reading to gain different methods of writing again. In my senior year of high school, my English teacher told my mom that I might as well look into a modeling career because I wasn't applying myself as best I could. After hearing those words from my mom, I started to really think about my future. Nothing seemed to be going my way until I watched a play written and performed by members of my church in the summer of 2008. That's when I brought out a piece of paper and a pencil and began writing. With in a month's time, I had completed my first play, and the story was phenomenal. From there, I began

writing more and more, until I extended my play into a story. But then, it was time for a change. I moved from my hometown, Barstow, California, to where I currently reside in La Verne, California. Here I worked at Wal-Mart as a receiving associate and then part of the asset protection team. I began writing poetry while at work: on break, lunch, or when I was at home because of my younger brother's influence, Demetri Kelley. Together we wrote an inspirational poetry book titled God's Words from this Generation, and it was published February 27, 2012, through CreateSpace. During that publishing process, I began writing my first story novel titled The Love from Just One on February 9, 2012. I finished writing that particular book on July 31, 2012, and I am excited for people of all ages to read it. Because the next chapter in my life has yet to be written, I won't stop working the gift within my hands that God has given.